Police!!!

Robert W. Chambers

TO LOUISE JOCELYN

All the pretty things you say,
All the pretty things you do
In your own delightful way
Make me fall in love with you,
Turning Autumn into May.

Every day is twice as gay
Just because of you, Louise!
Which is going some, you say?
In my dull, pedantic way
I am fashioning my lay
Just because I want to please.

Just because the things you say,
Just because the things you do
In your clever, charming way
Make me fall in love with you.
That is all, my dear, to-day.

R.W.C.
Christmas, 1915

CONTENTS

FOREWORD

Give me no gold nor palaces
Nor quarts of gems in chalices
Nor mention me in Who is Who
I'd rather roam abroad with you
Investigating sky and land,
Volcanoes, lakes, and glacial sand
I'd rather climb with all my legs
To find a nest of speckled eggs,
Or watch the spotted spider spin
Or see a serpent shed its skin!
Give me no star-and-garter blue!
I'd rather roam around with you.

Flatten me not with flattery!
Walk with me to the Battery,
And see in glassy tanks the seals,
The sturgeons, flounders, smelt and eels
Disport themselves in ichthyic curves—
And when it gets upon our nerves
Then, while our wabbling taxi honks
I'll tell you all about the Bronx,
Where captive wild things mope and stare
Through grills of steel that bar each lair
Doomed to imprisonment for life—
And you may go and take your wife.

Come to the Park[1] with me;
I'll show you crass stupidity
Which sentences the hawk and fox
To inactivity, and locks
The door of freedom on the lynx
Where puma pines and eagle stinks.
Never a slaver's fetid hold
Has held the misery untold
That crowds the great cats' kennels where
Their vacant eyes glare blank despair

---

[1] Central Park, filthiest, cruellest and most outrageous of zoological exhibitions.

Half crazed by sloth, half dazed by fear
All day, all night, year after year.

To the swift, clean things that cleave the air
To the swift, clean things that cleave the sea
To the swift, clean things that brave and dare
Forest and peak and prairie free,
A cage to craze and stifle and stun
And a fat man feeding a penny bun
And a she-one giggling, "Ain't it grand!"
As she drags a dirty-nosed brat by the hand.

PREFACE

On a beautiful day in spring as I was running as hard as I could run pursued by the New York police and a number of excited citizens, my mind, which becomes brilliantly active under physical exhilaration, began to work busily.

I thought about all sorts of things: I thought about hard times and financial depression and about our great President who is in a class all alone with himself and soon to become extinct; I thought about art and why there isn't any when it's talked about; I thought of macro-lepidoptera, of metagrammatism, monoliths, manicures, and monsoons.

And all the time I was running as fast as I could run; and the faster I ran the more things I thought about until my terrific pace set my brain whizzing like a wheel.

I felt no remorse at having published these memoirs of my life—which was why the police and populace were pursuing me, maddened to frenzy by the fearless revelation of mighty scientific truths in this little volume you are about to attempt to read. Ubicumque ars ostentatur, veritas abesse videtur!

I thought about it clearly, calmly, concisely as I fled. The maddened shouts of the prejudiced populace did not disturb me. Around and around the Metropolitan Museum of Art I ran; the inmates of that institution came out to watch me and they knew at a glance that I was one of them for they set up a clamor like a bunch of decoy ducks when one of their wild comrades comes whirling by.

"Police! Police!" they shouted; but I went careering on uptown, afraid only that the park squirrels might club together to corner me. There are corners in grain. Why not in—but let that pass.

I took the park wall in front of the great Mr. Carnegie's cottage at a single bound. He stood on his terrace and shouted, "Police!" He was quite logical.

The Equal Franchise Society was having a May party in the park near the Harlem Mere. They had chosen the Honorable William Jennings Bryan as Queen of the May. He wore low congress-gaiters and white socks; he was walking under a canopy, crowned with paper flowers, his hair curled over his coat collar, the tips of his fingers were suavely joined over his abdomen.

The moment he caught sight of me he shouted, "Police!"

He was right. The cabinet lacked only me.

And I might have consented to tarry—might have allowed

myself to be apprehended for political purposes, had not a nobler, holier, more imperative duty urged me northward still.

Though all Bloomingdale shouted, "Stop him!" and all Matteawan yelled, "Police!" I should not have consented to pause. Even the quackitudinous recognition spontaneously offered by the Metropolitan Museum had not been sufficient to decoy me to my fellows.

I knew, of course, that I could find a sanctuary and a welcome in many places—in almost any sectarian edifice, any club, any newspaper office, any of the great publishers', any school, any museum; I knew that I would be welcomed at Columbia University, at the annex to the Hall of Fame, in the Bishop's Palace on Morningside Heights—there were many places all ready to receive, understand and honour me.

For a sufficiently crippled intellect, for a still-born brain, for the intellectually aborted, there is always a place on some editorial, sectarian, or educational staff.

Try It!

But I had other ideas as I galloped northward. The voiceless summons of the most jealous of mistresses was making siren music in my ears. That coquettish jade, Science, was calling me by wireless, and I was responding with both legs.

And so, at last, I arrived at the Bronx Park and dashed into the Administration Building where everybody rose and cheered me to the echo.

I was at home at last, unterrified, undismayed, and ready again as always to dedicate my life to the service of Truth and to every caprice and whim of my immortal mistress, Science. But I don't want to marry her.

Magna est veritas! Sed major et longinquo reverentia.

POLICE!!!

Being a few deathless truths concerning several mysteries recently and scientifically unravelled by a modest servant of Science.

Quo quisque stultior, eo magis insolescit.

THE THIRD EYE

Although the man's back was turned toward me, I was uncomfortably conscious that he was watching me. How he could possibly be watching me while I stood directly behind him, I did not ask myself; yet, nevertheless, instinct warned me that I was being inspected; that somehow or other the man was staring at me as steadily as though he and I had been face to face and his faded, sea-green eyes were focussed upon me.

It was an odd sensation which persisted in spite of logic, and of which I could not rid myself. Yet the little waitress did not seem to share it. Perhaps she was not under his glassy inspection. But then, of course, I could not be either.

No doubt the nervous tension incident to the expedition was making me supersensitive and even morbid.

Our sail-boat rode the shallow torquoise-tinted waters at anchor, rocking gently just off the snowy coral reef on which we were now camping. The youthful waitress who, for economy's sake, wore her cap, apron, collar and cuffs over her dainty print dress, was seated by the signal fire writing in her diary. Sometimes she thoughtfully touched her pencil point with the tip of her tongue; sometimes she replenished the fire from a pile of dead mangrove branches heaped up on the coral reef beside her. Whatever she did she accomplished gracefully.

As for the man, Grue, his back remained turned toward us both and he continued, apparently, to scan the horizon for the sail which we all expected. And all the time I could not rid myself of the unpleasant idea that somehow or other he was looking at me, watching attentively the expression of my features and noting my every movement.

The smoke of our fire blew wide across leagues of shallow, sparkling water, or, when the wind veered, whirled back into our faces across the reef, curling and eddying among the standing mangroves like fog drifting.

Seated there near the fire, from time to time I swept the horizon with my marine glasses; but there was no sign of Kemper; no sail broke the far sweep of sky and water; nothing moved out there save when a wild duck took wing amid the dark raft of its companions to circle low above the ocean and settle at random, invisible again except when, at intervals, its white breast flashed in the sunshine.

Meanwhile the waitress had ceased to write in her diary and

now sat with the closed book on her knees and her pencil resting against her lips, gazing thoughtfuly at the back of Grue's head.

It was a ratty head of straight black hair, and looked greasy. The rest of him struck me as equally unkempt and dingy—a youngish man, lean, deeply bitten by the sun of the semi-tropics to a mahogany hue, and unusually hairy.

I don't mind a brawny, hairy man, but the hair on Grue's arms and chest was a rusty red, and like a chimpanzee's in texture, and sometimes a wildly absurd idea possessed me that the man needed it when he went about in the palm forests without his clothes.

But he was only a "poor white"—a "cracker" recruited from one of the reefs near Pelican Light, where he lived alone by fishing and selling his fish to the hotels at Heliatrope City. The sail-boat was his; he figured as our official guide on this expedition—an expedition which already had begun to worry me a great deal.

For it was, perhaps, the wildest goose chase and the most absurdly hopeless enterprise ever undertaken in the interest of science by the Bronx Park authorities.

Nothing is more dreaded by scientists than ridicule; and it was in spite of this terror of ridicule that I summoned sufficient courage to organize an exploring party and start out in search of something so extraordinary, so hitherto unheard of, that I had not dared reveal to Kemper by letter the object of my quest.

No, I did not care to commit myself to writing just yet; I had merely sent Kemper a letter to join me on Sting-ray Key.

He telegraphed me from Tampa that he would join me at the rendezvous; and I started directly from Bronx Park for Heliatrope City; arrived there in three days; found the waitress all ready to start with me; inquired about a guide and discovered the man Grue in his hut off Pelican Light; made my bargain with him; and set sail for Sting-ray Key, the most excited and the most nervous young man who ever had dared disaster in the sacred cause of science.

Everything was now at stake, my honour, reputation, career, fortune. For, as chief of the Anthropological Field Survey Department of the great Bronx Park Zoölogical Society, I was perfectly aware that no scientific reputation can survive ridicule.

Nevertheless, the die had been cast, the Rubicon crossed in a sail-boat containing one beachcombing cracker, one hotel waitress, a pile of camping kit and special utensils, and myself!

How was I going to tell Kemper? How was I going to confess to him that I was staking my reputation as an anthropologist upon a letter or two and a personal interview with a young girl—a waitress at the Hotel Gardenia in Heliatrope City?

I lowered my sea-glasses and glanced sideways at the waitress. She was still chewing the end of her pencil, reflectively.

She was a pretty girl, one Evelyn Grey, and had been a country school-teacher in Massachusetts until her health broke.

Florida was what she required; but that healing climate was possible to her only if she could find there a self-supporting position.

Also she had nourished an ambition for a postgraduate education, with further aspirations to a Government appointment in the Smithsonian Institute.

All very worthy, no doubt—in fact, particularly commendable because the wages she saved as waitress in a Florida hotel during the winter were her only means of support while studying for college examinations during the summer in Boston, where she lived.

Yet, although she was an inmate of Massachusetts, her face and figure would have ornamented any light-opera stage. I never looked at her but I thought so; and her cuffs and apron merely accentuated the delusion. Such ankles are seldom seen when the curtain rises after the overture. Odd that frivolous thoughts could flit through an intellect dedicated only to science!

The man, Grue, had not stirred from his survey of the Atlantic Ocean. He had a somewhat disturbing capacity for remaining motionless—like a stealthy and predatory bird which depends on immobility for aggressive and defensive existence.

The sea-wind fluttered his cotton shirt and trousers and the tattered brim of his straw hat. And always I felt as though he were watching me out of the back of his ratty head, through the ravelled straw brim that sagged over his neck.

The pretty waitress had now chewed the end of her pencil to a satisfactory pulp, and she was writing again in her diary, very intently, so that my cautious touch on her arm seemed to startle her.

Meeting her inquiring eyes I said in a low voice:

"I am not sure why, but I don't seem to care very much for that man, Grue. Do you?"

She glanced at the water's edge, where Grue stood, immovable, his back still turned to us.

"I never liked him," she said under her breath.

"Why?" I asked cautiously.

She merely shrugged her shoulders. She did it gracefully.

I said:

"Have you any particular reason for disliking him?"

"He's dirty."

"He looks dirty, yet every day he goes into the sea and swims about. He ought to be clean enough."

She thought for a moment, then:

"He seems, somehow, to be fundamentally unclean—I don't mean that he doesn't wash himself. But there are certain sorts of animals and birds and other creatures from which one instinctively shrinks—not, perhaps, because they are materially unclean—"

"I understand," I said. After a silence I added: "Well, there's no chance now of sending him back, even if I were inclined to do so. He appears to be familiar with these latitudes. I don't suppose we could find a better man for our purpose. Do you?"

"No. He was a sponge fisher once, I believe."

"Did he tell you so?"

"No. But yesterday, when you took the boat and cruised to the south, I sat writing here and keeping up the fire. And I saw Grue climbing about among the mangroves over the water in a most uncanny way; and two snake-birds sat watching him, and they never moved.

"He didn't seem to see them; his back was toward them. And then, all at once, he leaped backward at them where they sat on a mangrove, and he got one of them by the neck—"

"What!"

The girl nodded.

"By the neck," she repeated, "and down they went into the water. And what do you suppose happened?"

"I can't imagine," said I with a grimace.

"Well, Grue went under, still clutching the squirming, flapping bird; and he stayed under."

"Stayed under the water?"

"Yes, longer than any sponge diver I ever heard of. And I was becoming frightened when the bloody bubbles and feathers began to come up—"

"What was he doing under water?"

"He must have been tearing the bird to pieces. Oh, it was quite unpleasant, I assure you, Mr. Smith. And when he came up and looked at me out of those very vitreous eyes he resembled something horridly amphibious.... And I felt rather sick and dizzy."

"He's got to stop that sort of thing!" I said angrily. "Snake-birds are harmless and I won't have him killing them in that barbarous fashion. I've warned him already to let birds alone. I don't know how he catches them or why he kills them. But he seems to have a mania for doing it—"

I was interrupted by Grue's soft and rather pleasant voice from the water's edge, announcing a sail on the horizon. He did not turn when speaking.

The next moment I made out the sail and focussed my glasses on it.

"It's Professor Kemper," I announced presently.

"I'm so glad," remarked Evelyn Grey.

I don't know why it should have suddenly occurred to me, apropos of nothing, that Billy Kemper was unusually handsome. Or why I should have turned and looked at the pretty waitress—except that she was, perhaps, worth gazing upon from a purely non-scientific point of view. In fact, to a man not entirely absorbed in scientific research and not passionately and irrevocably wedded to his profession, her violet-blue eyes and rather sweet mouth might have proved disturbing.

As I was thinking about this she looked up at me and smiled.

"It's a good thing," I thought to myself, "that I am irrevocably wedded to my profession." And I gazed fixedly across the Atlantic Ocean.

There was scarcely sufficient breeze of a steady character to bring Kemper to Sting-ray Key; but he got out his sweeps when I hailed him and came in at a lively clip, anchoring alongside of our boat and leaping ashore with that unnecessary dash and abandon which women find pleasing.

Glancing sideways at my waitress through my spectacles, I found her looking into a small hand mirror and patting her hair with one slim and suntanned hand.

When Professor Kemper landed on the coral he shot a curious look at Grue, and then came striding across the reef to me.

"Hello, Smithy!" he said, holding out his hand. "Here I am, you see! Now what's up—"

Just then Evelyn Grey got up from her seat beside the fire; and Kemper turned and gazed at her with every symptom of unfeigned approbation.

I introduced him. Evelyn Grey seemed a trifle indifferent. A good-looking man doesn't last long with a clever woman. I smiled to myself, polishing my spectacles gleefully. Yet, I had no idea why I was smiling.

We three people turned and walked toward the comb of the reef. A solitary palm represented the island's vegetation, except, of course, for the water-growing mangroves.

I asked Miss Grey to precede us and wait for us under the palm; and she went forward in that light-footed way of hers which, to any non-scientific man, might have been a trifle disturbing. It had no effect upon me. Besides, I was looking at Grue, who had gone to the fire and was evidently preparing to fry our evening meal of fish and rice. I didn't like to have him cook, but I wasn't going to do it myself; and my pretty waitress didn't know how to cook anything more complicated than beans. We had no beans.

Kemper said to me:

"Why on earth did you bring a waitress?"

"Not to wait on table," I replied, amused. "I'll explain her later. Meanwhile, I merely want to say that you need not remain with this expedition if you don't want to. It's optional with you."

"That's a funny thing to say!"

"No, not funny; sad. The truth is that if I fail I'll be driven into obscurity by the ridicule of my brother scientists the world over. I had to tell them at the Bronx what I was going after. Every man connected with the society attempted to dissuade me, saying that the whole thing was absurd and that my reputation would suffer if I engaged in such a ridiculous quest. So when you hear what that girl and I are after out here in the semi-tropics, and when you are in possession of the only evidence I have to justify my credulity, if you want to go home, go. Because I don't wish to risk your reputation as a scientist unless you choose to risk it yourself."

He regarded me curiously, then his eyes strayed toward the palm-tree which Evelyn Grey was now approaching.

"All right," he said briefly, "let's hear what's up."

So we moved forward to rejoin the girl, who had already seated herself under the tree.

She looked very attractive in her neat cuffs, tiny cap, and pink print gown, as we approached her.

"Why does she dress that way?" asked Kemper, uneasily.

"Economy. She desires to use up the habiliments of a service which there will be no necessity for her to reënter if this expedition proves successful."

"Oh. But Smithy—"

"What?"

"Was it—moral—to bring a waitress?"

"Perfectly," I replied sharply. "Science knows no sex!"

"I don't understand how a waitress can be scientific," he muttered, "and there seems to be no question about her possessing plenty of sex—"

"If that girl's conclusions are warranted," I interrupted coldly, "she is a most intelligent and clever person. I think they are warranted. If you don't, you may go home as soon as you like."

I glanced at him; he was smiling at her with that strained politeness which alters the natural expression of men in the imminence of a conversation with a new and pretty woman.

I often wonder what particular combination of facial muscles are brought into play when that politely receptive expression transforms the normal and masculine features into a fixed simper.

When Kemper and I had seated ourselves, I calmly cut short the small talk in which he was already indulging, and to which, I am sorry to say, my pretty waitress was beginning to respond. I had scarcely thought it of her—but that's neither here nor there—and I invited her to recapitulate the circumstances which had resulted in our present foregathering here on this strip of coral in the Atlantic Ocean.

She did so very modestly and without embarrassment, stating the case and reviewing the evidence so clearly and so simply that I could see how every word she uttered was not only amazing but also convincing Kemper.

When she had ended he asked a few questions very seriously:

"Granted," he said, "that the pituitary gland represents what we assume it represents, how much faith is to be placed in the testimony of a Seminole Indian?"

"A Seminole Indian," she replied, "has seldom or never been known to lie. And where a whole tribe testify alike the truth of what they assert can not be questioned."

"How did you make them talk? They are a sullen, suspicious people, haughty, uncommunicative, seldom even replying to an ordinary question from a white man."

"They consider me one of them."

"Why?" he asked in surprise.

"I'll tell you why. It came about through a mere accident. I was waitress at the hotel; it happened to be my afternoon off; so I went down to the coquina dock to study. I study in my leisure moments, because I wish to fit myself for a college examination."

Her charming face became serious; she picked up the hem of her apron and continued to pleat it slowly and with precision as she talked:

"There was a Seminole named Tiger-tail sitting there, his feet dangling above his moored canoe, evidently waiting for the tide to turn before he went out to spear crayfish. I merely noticed he was sitting there in the sunshine, that's all. And then I opened my mythology book and turned to the story of Argus, on which I was reading up.

"And this is what happened: there was a picture of the death of Argus, facing the printed page which I was reading—the well-known picture where Juno is holding the head of the decapitated monster— and I had read scarcely a dozen words in the book before the Seminole beside me leaned over and placed his forefinger squarely upon the head of Argus.

"'Who?' he demanded.

"I looked around good-humoredly and was surprised at the evident excitement of the Indian. They're not excitable, you know.

"'That,' said I, 'is a Greek gentleman named Argus.' I suppose he thought I meant a Minorcan, for he nodded. Then, without further comment, he placed his finger on Juno.

"'Who?' he inquired emphatically.

"I said flippantly: 'Oh, that's only my aunt, Juno.'

"'Aunty of you?'

"'Yes.'

"'She kill 'um Three-eye?'

"Argus had been depicted with three eyes.

"'Yes,' I said, 'my Aunt Juno had Argus killed.'

"'Why kill 'um?'

"'Well, Aunty needed his eyes to set in the tails of the peacocks which drew her automobile. So when they cut off the head of Argus my aunt had the eyes taken out; and that's a picture of how she set them into the peacock.'

"'Aunty of you?' he repeated.

"'Certainly,' I said gravely; 'I am a direct descendant of the Goddess of Wisdom. That's why I'm always studying when you see me down on the dock here.'

"'You Seminole!' he said emphatically.

"'Seminole,' I repeated, puzzled.

"'You Seminole! Aunty Seminole—you Seminole!'

"'Why, Tiger-tail?'

"'Seminole hunt Three-eye long time—hundred, hundred year—hunt 'um Three-eye, kill 'um Three-eye.'

"'You say that for hundreds of years the Seminoles have hunted a creature with three eyes?'

"'Sure! Hunt 'um now!'

"'Now?'

"'Sure!'

"'But, Tiger-tail, if the legends of your people tell you that the Seminoles hunted a creature with three eyes hundreds of years ago, certainly no such three-eyed creatures remain today?'

"'Some.'

"'What! Where?'

"'Black Bayou.'

"'Do you mean to tell me that a living creature with three eyes still inhabits the forests of Black Bayou?'

"'Sure. Me see 'um. Me kill 'um three-eye man.'

"'You have killed a man who had three eyes?'

"'Sure!'

"'A man? With three eyes?'

"'Sure.'"

The pretty waitress, excitedly engrossed in her story, was unconsciously acting out the thrilling scene of her dialogue with the Indian, even imitating his voice and gestures. And Kemper and I listened and watched her breathlessly, fascinated by her lithe and supple grace as well as by the astounding story she was so frankly unfolding with the consummate artlessness of a natural actress.

She turned her flushed face to us:

"I made up my mind," she said, "that Tiger-tail's story was worth investigating. It was perfectly easy for me to secure corroboration, because that Seminole went back to his Everglade camp and told every one of his people that I was a white Seminole because my ancestors also hunted the three-eyed man and nobody except a Seminole could know that such a thing as a three-eyed man existed.

"So, the next afternoon off, I embarked in Tiger-tail's canoe and he took me to his camp. And there I talked to his people, men and women, questioning, listening, putting this and that together, trying to discover some foundation for their persistent statements concerning men, still living in the jungles of Black Bayou, who had three eyes instead of two.

"All told the same story; all asserted that since the time their records ran the Seminoles had hunted and slain every three-eyed man they could catch; and that as long as the Seminoles had lived in the Everglades the three-eyed men had lived in the forests beyond Black Bayou."

She paused, dramatically, cooling her cheeks in her palms and looking from Kemper to me with eyes made starry by excitement.

"And what do you think!" she continued, under her breath. "To prove what they said they brought for my inspection a skull. And then two more skulls like the first one.

"Every skull had been painted with Spanish red; the coarse black hair still stuck to the scalps. And, behind, just over where the pituitary gland is situated, was a hollow, bony orbit—unmistakably the socket of a third eye!"

"W-where are those skulls?" demanded Kemper, in a voice not entirely under control.

"They wouldn't part with one of them. I tried every possible persuasion. On my own responsibility, and even before I communicated with Mr. Smith—" turning toward me, "—I offered them twenty thousand dollars for a single skull, staking my word of honour that the Bronx Museum would pay that sum.

"It was useless. Not only do the Seminoles refuse to part with one of those skulls, but I have also learned that I am the first person with a white skin who has ever even heard of their existence—so profoundly have these red men of the Everglades guarded their secret through centuries."

After a silence Kemper, rather pale, remarked:

"This is a most astonishing business, Miss Grey."

"What do you think about it?" I demanded. "Is it not worth while for us to explore Black Bayou?"

He nodded in a dazed sort of way, but his gaze remained riveted on the girl. Presently he said:

"Why does Miss Grey go?"

She turned in surprise:

"Why am I going? But it is my discovery—my contribution to science, isn't it?"

"Certainly!" we exclaimed warmly and in unison. And Kemper added: "I was only thinking of the dangers and hardships. Smith and I could do the actual work—"

"Oh!" she cried in quick protest, "I wouldn't miss one moment of the excitement, one pain, one pang! I love it! It would simply break my heart not to share every chance, hazard, danger of this expedition—every atom of hope, excitement, despair, uncertainty— and the ultimate success—the unsurpassable thrill of exultation in the final instant of triumph!"

She sprang to her feet in a flash of uncontrollable enthusiasm, and stood there, aglow with courage and resolution, making a highly agreeable picture in her apron and cuffs, the sea wind fluttering the bright tendrils of her hair under her dainty cap.

We got to our feet much impressed; and now absolutely convinced that there did exist, somewhere, descendants of prehistoric men in whom the third eye—placed in the back of the head for purposes of defensive observation—had not become obsolete and reduced to the traces which we know only as the pituitary body or pituitary gland.

Kemper and I were, of course, aware that in the insect world the ocelli served the same purpose that the degenerate pituitary body once served in the occiput of man.

As we three walked slowly back to the campfire, where our evening meal was now ready, Evelyn Grey, who walked between us, told us what she knew about the hunting of these three-eyed men by the Seminoles—how intense was the hatred of the Indians for these people, how murderously they behaved toward any one of them whom they could track down and catch.

"Tiger-tail told me," she went on, "that in all probability the strange race was nearing extinction, but that all had not yet been exterminated because now and then, when hunting along Black Bayou, traces of living three-eyed men were still found by him and his people.

"No later than last week Tiger-tail himself had startled one of these strange denizens of Black Bayou from a meal of fish; and had heard him leap through the bushes and plunge into the water. It appears that centuries of persecution have made these three-eyed men partly amphibious—that is, capable of filling their lungs with air and remaining under water almost as long as a turtle."

"That's impossible!" said Kemper bluntly.

"I thought so myself," she said with a smile, "until Tiger-tail told me a little more about them. He says that they can breathe through the pores of their skins; that their bodies are covered with a thick, silky hair, and that when they dive they carry down with them enough air to form a sort of skin over them, so that under water their bodies appear to be silver-plated."

"Good Lord!" faltered Kemper. "That is a little too much!"

"Yet," said I, "that is exactly what air-breathing water beetles do. The globules of air, clinging to the body-hairs, appear to silver-plate them; and they can remain below indefinitely, breathing through spiracles. Doubtless the skin pores of these men have taken on the character of spiracles."

"You know," he said in a curious, flat voice, which sounded like the tones of a partly stupified man, "this whole business is so grotesque—apparently so wildly absurd—that it's having a sort of nightmare effect on me." And, dropping his voice to a whisper close to my ear: "Good heavens!" he said. "Can you reconcile such a creature as we are starting out to hunt, with anything living known to science?"

"No," I replied in guarded tones. "And there are moments, Kemper, since I have come into possession of Miss Grey's story, when I find myself seriously doubting my own sanity."

"I'm doubting mine, now," he whispered, "only that girl is so fresh and wholesome and human and sane—"

"She is a very clever girl," I said.

"And really beautiful!"

"She is intelligent," I remarked. There was a chill in my tone which doubtless discouraged Kemper, for he ventured nothing further concerning her superficially personal attractions.

After all, if any questions of priority were to arise, the pretty waitress was my discovery. And in the scientific world it is an inflexible rule that he who first discovers any particular specimen of any species whatever is first entitled to describe and comment upon that specimen without interference or unsolicited advice from anybody.

Maybe there was in my eye something that expressed as much. For when Kemper caught my cold gaze fixed upon him he winced and looked away like a reproved setter dog who knew better. Which also, for the moment, put an end to the rather gay and frivolous line of small talk which he had again begun with the pretty waitress.

I was exceedingly surprised at Professor William Henry Kemper, D.F.

As we approached the campfire the loathsome odour of frying mullet saluted my nostrils.

Kemper, glancing at Grue, said aside to me:

"That's an odd-looking fellow. What is he? Minorcan?"

"Oh, just a beachcomber. I don't know what he is. He strikes me as dirty—though he can't be so, physically. I don't like him and I don't know why. And I wish we'd engaged somebody else to guide us."

Toward dawn something awoke me and I sat up in my blanket under the moon. But my leg had not been pulled.

Kemper snored at my side. In her little dog-tent the pretty waitress probably was fast asleep. I knew it because the string she had tied to one of her ornamental ankles still lay across the ground convenient to my hand. In any emergency I had only to pull it to awake her.

A similar string, tied to my ankle, ran parallel to hers and disappeared under the flap of her tent. This was for her to pull if she liked. She had never yet pulled it. Nor I the other. Nevertheless I truly felt that these humble strings were, in a subtler sense, ties that bound us together. No wonder Kemper's behaviour had slightly irritated me.

I looked up at the silver moon; I glanced at Kemper's unlovely bulk, swathed in a blanket; I contemplated the dog-tent with, perhaps, that slight trace of sentiment which a semi-tropical moon is likely to inspire even in a jellyfish. And suddenly I remembered Grue and looked for him.

He was accustomed to sleep in his boat, but I did not see him in either of the boats. Here and there were a few lumpy shadows in the moonlight, but none of them was Grue lying prone on the ground. Where the devil had he gone?

Cautiously I untied my ankle string, rose in my pajamas, stepped into my slippers, and walked out through the moonlight.

There was nothing to hide Grue, no rocks or vegetation except the solitary palm on the back-bone of the reef.

I walked as far as the tree and looked up into the arching

fronds. Nobody was up there. I could see the moonlit sky through the fronds. Nor was Grue lying asleep anywhere on the other side of the coral ridge.

And suddenly I became aware of all my latent distrust and dislike for the man. And the vigour of my sentiments surprised me because I really had not understood how deep and thorough my dislike had been.

Also, his utter disappearance struck me as uncanny. Both boats were there; and there were many leagues of sea to the nearest coast.

Troubled and puzzled I turned and walked back to the dead embers of the fire. Kemper had merely changed the timbre of his snore to a whistling aria, which at any other time would have enraged me. Now, somehow, it almost comforted me.

Seated on the shore I looked out to sea, racking my brains for an explanation of Grue's disappearance. And while I sat there racking them, far out on the water a little flock of ducks suddenly scattered and rose with frightened quackings and furiously beating wings.

For a moment I thought I saw a round, dark object on the waves where the flock had been.

And while I sat there watching, up out of the sea along the reef to my right crawled a naked, dripping figure holding a dead duck in his mouth.

Fascinated, I watched it, recognising Grue with his ratty black hair all plastered over his face.

Whether he caught sight of me or not, I don't know; but he suddenly dropped the dead duck from his mouth, turned, and dived under water.

It was a grim and horrid species of sport or pastime, this amphibious business of his, catching wild birds and dragging them about as though he were an animal.

Evidently he was ashamed of himself, for he had dropped the duck. I watched it floating by on the waves, its head under water. Suddenly something jerked it under, a fish perhaps, for it did not come up and float again, as far as I could see.

When I went back to camp Grue lay apparently asleep on the north side of the fire. I glanced at him in disgust and crawled into my tent.

The next day Evelyn Grey awoke with a headache and kept her tent. I had all I could do to prevent Kemper from prescribing for her. I did that myself, sitting beside her and testing her pulse for hours at a time, while Kemper took one of Grue's grains and went off into the mangroves and speared grunt and eels for a chowder which he said he knew how to concoct.

Toward afternoon the pretty waitress felt much better, and I warned Kemper and Grue that we should sail for Black Bayou after dinner.

Dinner was a mess, as usual, consisting of fried mullet and rice, and a sort of chowder in which the only ingredients I recognised were sections of crayfish.

After we had finished and had withdrawn from the fire, Grue scraped every remaining shred of food into a kettle and went for it. To see him feed made me sick, so I rejoined Miss Grey and Kemper, who had found a green cocoanut and were alternately deriving nourishment from the milk inside it.

Somehow or other there seemed to me a certain levity about that performance, and it made me uncomfortable; but I managed to smile a rather sickly smile when they offered me a draught, and I took a pull at the milk—I don't exactly know why, because I don't like it. But the moon was up over the sea, now, and the dusk was languorously balmy, and I didn't care to leave those two drinking milk out of the same cocoanut under a tropic moon.

Not that my interest in Evelyn Grey was other than scientific. But after all it was I who had discovered her.

We sailed as soon as Grue, gobbling and snuffling, had cleaned up the last crumb of food. Kemper blandly offered to take Miss Grey into his boat, saying that he feared my boat was overcrowded, what with the paraphernalia, the folding cages, Grue, Miss Grey, and myself.

I sat on that suggestion, but offered to take my own tiller and lend him Grue. He couldn't wriggle out of it, seeing that his alleged motive had been the overcrowding of my boat, but he looked rather sick when Grue went aboard his boat.

As for me, I hoisted sail with something so near a chuckle that it surprised me; and I looked at Evelyn Grey to see whether she had noticed the unseemly symptom.

Apparently she had not. She sat forward, her eyes fixed soulfully upon the moon. Had I been dedicated to any profession except a scientific one—but let that pass.

Grue in Kemper's sail-boat led, and my boat followed out into the silvery and purple dusk, now all sparkling under the high lustre of the moon.

Dimly I saw vast rafts of wild duck part and swim leisurely away to port and starboard, leaving a glittering lane of water for us to sail through; into the scintillant night from the sea sprang mullet, silvery, quivering, falling back into the wash with a splash.

Here and there in the moonlight steered ominous black triangles, circling us, leading us, sheering across bow and flashing wake, all phosphorescent with lambent sea-fire—the fins of great sharks.

"You need have no fear," said I to the pretty waitress.

She said nothing.

"Of course if you are afraid," I added, "perhaps you might care to change your seat."

There was room in the stern where I sat.

"Do you think there is any danger?" she asked.

"From sharks?"

"Yes."

"Reaching up and biting you?"

"Yes."

"Oh, I don't really suppose there is," I said, managing to convey the idea, I am ashamed to say, that the catastrophe was a possibility.

She came over and seated herself beside me. I was very much ashamed of myself, but I could not repress a triumphant glance ahead at the other boat, where Kemper sat huddled forward, evidently bored to extinction.

Every now and then I could see him turn and crane his neck as though in an effort to distinguish what was going on in our boat.

There was nothing going on, absolutely nothing. The moon was magnificent; and I think the pretty waitress must have been a little tired, for her head drooped and nodded at moments, even while I was talking to her about a specimen of Euplectilla speciosa on which I had written a monograph. So she must have been really tired, for the subject was interesting.

"You won't incommode my operations with sheet and tiller," I said to her kindly, "if you care to rest your head against my shoulder."

Evidently she was very tired, for she did so, and closed her eyes.

After a while, fearing that she might fall over backward into the sea—but let that pass.... I don't know whether or not Kemper could distinguish anything aboard our boat. He craned his head enough to twist it off his neck.

To be so utterly, so blindly devoted to science is a great safeguard for a man. Single-mindedness, however, need not induce atrophy of every humane impulse. I drew the pretty waitress closer—not that the night was cold, but it might become so. Changes in the tropics come swiftly. It is well to be prepared.

Her cheek felt very soft against my shoulder. There seemed to be a faint perfume about her hair. It really was odd how subtly fragrant she seemed to be—almost, perhaps, a matter of scientific interest.

Her hands did not seem to be chilled; they did seem unusually smooth and soft.

I said to her: "When at home, I suppose your mother tucks you in; doesn't she?"

"Yes," she nodded sleepily.

"And what does she do then?" said I, with something of that ponderous playfulness with which I make scientific jokes at a meeting of the Bronx Anthropological Association, when I preside.

"She kisses me and turns out the light," said Evelyn Grey, innocently.

I don't know how much Kemper could distinguish. He kept dodging about and twisting his head until I really thought it would come off, unless it had been screwed on like the top of a piano stool.

A few minutes later he fired his pistol twice; and Evelyn sat up. I never knew why he fired; he never offered any explanation.

Toward midnight I could hear the roar of breakers on our starboard bow. Evelyn heard them, too, and sat up inquiringly.

"Grue has found the inlet to Black Bayou, I suppose," said I.

And it proved to be the case, for, with the surf thundering on either hand, we sailed into a smoothly flowing inlet through which the flood tide was running between high dunes all sparkling in the moonlight and crowned with shadowy palms.

Occasionally I heard noises ahead of us from the other boat, as though Kemper was trying to converse with us, but as his apropos was as unintelligible as it was inopportune, I pretended not to hear him. Besides, I had all I could do to manoeuvre the tiller and prevent Evelyn Grey from falling off backward into the bayou. Besides, it is not customary to converse with the man at the helm.

After a while—during which I seemed to distinguish in Kemper's voice a quality that rhymes with his name—his tones varied through phases all the way from irony to exasperation. After a while he gave it up and took to singing.

There was a moon, and I suppose he thought he had a voice. It didn't strike me so. After several somewhat melancholy songs, he let off his pistol two or three times and then subsided into silence.

I didn't care; neither his songs nor his shots interrupted—but let that pass, also.

We were now sailing into the forest through pool after pool of interminable lagoons, startling into unseen and clattering flight hundreds of waterfowl. I could feel the wind from their whistling wings in the darkness, as they drove by us out to sea. It seemed to startle the pretty waitress. It is a solemn thing to be responsible for a pretty girl's peace of mind. I reassured her continually, perhaps a trifle nervously. But there were no more pistol shots. Perhaps Kemper had used up his cartridges.

We were still drifting along under drooping sails, borne inland almost entirely by the tide, when the first pale, watery, gray light streaked the east. When it grew a little lighter, Evelyn sat up; all danger of sharks being over. Also, I could begin to see what was going on in the other boat. Which was nothing remarkable; Kemper slumped against the mast, his head turned in our direction; Grue sat at the helm, motionless, his tattered straw hat sagging on his neck.

When the sun rose, I called out cheerily to Kemper, asking him how he had passed the night. Evelyn also raised her head, pausing while bringing her disordered hair under discipline, to listen to his reply.

But he merely mumbled something. Perhaps he was still sleepy.

As for me, I felt exceedingly well; and when Grue turned his craft in shore, I did so, too; and when, under the overhanging foliage of the forest, the nose of my boat grated on the sand, I rose and crossed the deck with a step distinctly frolicsome.

Kemper seemed distant and glum; Evelyn Grey spoke to him shyly now and then, and I noticed she looked at him only when he was gazing elsewhere than at her. She had a funny, conciliatory air with him, half ashamed, partly humorous and amused, as though something about Kemper's sulky ill-humour was continually making tiny inroads on her gravity.

Some mullet had jumped into the two boats—half a dozen during our moonlight voyage—and these were now being fried with rice for us by Grue. Lord! How I hated to eat them!

After we had finished breakfast, Grue, as usual, did everything to the remainder except to get into the fry-pan with both feet; and as usual he sickened me.

When he'd cleaned up everything, I sent him off into the forest to find a dry shell-mound for camping purposes; then I made fast both boats, and Kemper and I carried ashore our paraphernalia, spare batterie-de-cuisine, firearms, fishing tackle, spears, harpoons, grains, oars, sails, spars, folding cage—everything with which a strictly scientific expedition is usually burdened.

Evelyn was washing her face in the crystal waters of a branch that flowed into the lagoon from under the live-oaks. She looked very pretty doing it, like a naiad or dryad scrubbing away at her forest toilet.

It was, in fact, such a pretty spectacle that I was going over to sit beside her while she did it, but Kemper started just when I was going to, and I turned away. Some men invariably do the wrong thing. But a handsome man doesn't last long with a pretty girl.

I was thinking of this as I stood contemplating an alligator slide, when Grue came back saying that the shore on which we had landed was the termination of a shell-mound, and that it was the only dry place he had found.

So I bade him pitch our tents a few feet back from the shore; and stood watching him while he did so, one eye reverting occasionally to Evelyn Grey and Kemper. They both were seated cross-legged beside the branch, and they seemed to be talking a great deal and rather earnestly. I couldn't quite understand what they found to talk about so earnestly and volubly all of a sudden, inasmuch as they had heretofore exchanged very few observations during a most brief and formal acquaintance, dating only from sundown the day before.

Grue set up our three tents, carried the luggage inland, and then hung about for a while until the vast shadow of a vulture swept across the trees.

I never saw such an indescribable expression on a human face as I saw on Grue's as he looked up at the huge, unclean bird. His vitreous eyes fairly glittered; the corners of his mouth quivered and grew wet; and to my astonishment he seemed to emit a low, mewing noise.

"What the devil are you doing?" I said impulsively, in my amazement and disgust.

He looked at me, his eyes still glittering, the corners of his mouth still wet; but the curious sounds had ceased.

"What?" he asked.

"Nothing. I thought you spoke." I didn't know what else to say.

He made no reply. Once, when I had partly turned my head, I was aware that he was warily turning his to look at the vulture, which had alighted heavily on the ground near the entrails and heads of the mullet, where he had cast them on the dead leaves.

I walked over to where Evelyn Grey and Kemper sat so busily conversing; and their volubility ceased as they glanced up and saw me approaching. Which phenomenon both perplexed and displeased me.

I said:

"This is the Black Bayou forest, and we have the most serious business of our lives before us. Suppose you and I start out, Kemper, and see if there are any traces of what we are after in the neighborhood of our camp."

"Do you think it safe to leave Miss Grey alone in camp?" he asked gravely.

I hadn't thought of that:

"No, of course not," I said. "Grue can stay."

"I don't need anybody," she said quickly. "Anyway, I'm rather afraid of Grue."

"Afraid of Grue?" I repeated.

"Not exactly afraid. But he's—unpleasant."

"I'll remain with Miss Grey," said Kemper politely.

"Oh," she exclaimed, "I couldn't ask that. It is true that I feel a little tired and nervous, but I can go with you and Mr. Smith and Grue—"

I surveyed Kemper in cold perplexity. As chief of the expedition, I couldn't very well offer to remain with Evelyn Grey, but I didn't propose that Kemper should, either.

"Take Grue," he suggested, "and look about the woods for a while. Perhaps after dinner Miss Grey may feel sufficiently rested to join us."

"I am sure," she said, "that a few hours' rest in camp will set me on my feet. All I need is rest. I didn't sleep very soundly last night."

I felt myself growing red, and I looked away from them both.

"Oh," said Kemper, in apparent surprise, "I thought you had slept soundly all night long."

"Nobody," said I, "could have slept very pleasantly during that musical performance of yours."

"Were you singing?" she asked innocently of Kemper.

"He was singing when he wasn't firing off his pistol," I remarked. "No wonder you couldn't sleep with any satisfaction to yourself."

Grue had disappeared into the forest; I stood watching for him to come out again. After a few minutes I heard a furious but distant noise of flapping; the others also heard it; and we listened in silence, wondering what it was.

"It's Grue killing something," faltered Evelyn Grey, turning a trifle pale.

"Confound it!" I exclaimed. "I'm going to stop that right now."

Kemper rose and followed me as I started for the woods; but as we passed the beached boats Grue appeared from among the trees.

"Where have you been?" I demanded.

"In the woods."

"Doing what?"

"Nothing."

There was a bit of down here and there clinging to his cotton shirt and trousers, and one had caught and stuck at the corner of his mouth.

"See here, Grue," I said, "I don't want you to kill any birds except for camp purposes. Why do you try to catch and kill birds?"

"I don't."

I stared at the man and he stared back at me out of his glassy eyes.

"You mean to say that you don't, somehow or other, manage to catch and kill birds?"

"No, I don't."

There was nothing further for me to say unless I gave him the lie. I didn't care to do that, needing his services.

Evelyn Grey had come up to join us; there was a brief silence; we all stood looking at Grue; and he looked back at us out of his pale, washed-out, and unblinking eyes.

"Grue," I said, "I haven't yet explained to you the object of this expedition to Black Bayou. Now, I'll tell you what I want. But first let me ask you a question or two. You know the Black Bayou forests, don't you?"

"Yes."

"Did you ever see anything unusual in these forests?"

"No."

"Are you sure?"

The man stared at us, one after another. Then he said:

"What are you looking for in Black Bayou?"

"Something very curious, very strange, very unusual. So strange and unusual, in fact, that the great Zoölogical Society of the Bronx in New York has sent me down here at the head of this expedition to search the forests of Black Bayou."

"For what?" he demanded, in a dull, accentless voice.

"For a totally new species of human being, Grue. I wish to catch one and take it back to New York in that folding cage."

His green eyes had grown narrow as though sun-dazzled. Kemper had stepped behind us into the woods and was now busy setting up the folding cage. Grue remained motionless.

"I am going to offer you," I said, "the sum of one thousand dollars in gold if you can guide us to a spot where we may see this hitherto unknown species—a creature which is apparently a man but which has, in the back of his head, a third eye—"

I paused in amazement: Grue's cheeks had suddenly puffed out and were quivering; and from the corners of his slitted mouth he was emitting a whimpering sound like the noise made by a low-circling pigeon.

"Grue!" I cried. "What's the matter with you?"

"What is he doing?" screamed Grue, quivering from head to foot, but not turning around.

"Who?" I cried.

"The man behind me!"

"Professor Kemper? He's setting up the folding cage—"

With a screech that raised my hair, Grue whipped out his murderous knife and hurled himself backward at Kemper, but the latter shrank aside behind the partly erected cage, and Grue whirled around, snarling, hacking, and even biting at the wood frame and steel bars.

And then occurred a thing so horrid that it sickened me to the pit of my stomach; for the man's sagging straw hat had fallen off, and there, in the back of his head, through the coarse, black, ratty hair, I saw a glassy eye glaring at me.

"Kemper!" I shouted. "He's got a third eye! He's one of them! Knock him flat with your riflestock!" And I seized a shot-gun from the top of the baggage bundle on the ground beside me, and leaped at Grue, aiming a terrific blow at him.

But the glassy eye in the back of his head was watching me between the clotted strands of hair, and he dodged both Kemper and me, swinging his heavy knife in circles and glaring at us both out of the front and back of his head.

Kemper seized him by his arm, but Grue's shirt came off, and I saw his entire body was as furry as an ape's. And all the while he was snapping at us and leaping hither and thither to avoid our blows; and from the corners of his puffed cheeks he whined and whimpered and mewed through the saliva foam.

"Keep him from the water!" I panted, following him with clubbed shot-gun; and as I advanced I almost stepped on a soiled heap of foulness—the dead buzzard which he had caught and worried to death with his teeth.

Suddenly he threw his knife at my head, hurling it backward; dodged, screeched, and bounded by me toward the shore of the lagoon, where the pretty waitress was standing, petrified.

For one moment I thought he had her, but she picked up her skirts, ran for the nearest boat, and seized a harpoon; and in his fierce eagerness to catch her he leaped clear over the boat and fell with a splash into the lagoon.

As Kemper and I sprang aboard and looked over into the water, we could see him going down out of reach of a harpoon; and his body seemed to be silver-plated, flashing and glittering like a burnished eel, so completely did the skin of air envelope him, held there by the fur that covered him.

And, as he rested for a moment on the bottom, deep down through the clear waters of the lagoon where he lay prone, I could see, as the current stirred his long, black hair, the third eye looking up at us, glassy, unwinking, horrible.

A bubble or two, like globules of quicksilver, were detached from the burnished skin of air that clothed him, and came glittering upward.

Suddenly there was a flash; a flurrying cloud of blue mud; and Grue was gone.

After a long while I turned around in the muteness of my despair. And slowly froze.

For the pretty waitress, becomingly pale, was gathered in Kemper's arms, her cheek against his shoulder. Neither seemed to be aware of me.

"Darling," he said, in the imbecile voice of a man in love, "why do you tremble so when I am here to protect you? Don't you love and trust me?"

"Oo—h—yes," she sighed, pressing her cheek closer to his shoulder.

I shoved my hands into my pockets, passed them without noticing them, and stepped ashore.

And there I sat down under a tree, with my back toward them, all alone and face to face with the greatest grief of my life.

But which it was—the loss of her or the loss of Grue, I had not yet made up my mind.

THE IMMORTAL

I

As everybody knows, the great majority of Americans, upon reaching the age of natural selection, are elected to the American Institute of Arts and Ethics, which is, so to speak, the Ellis Island of the Academy.

Occasionally a general mobilization of the Academy is ordered and, from the teeming population of the Institute, a new Immortal is selected for the American Academy of Moral Endeavor by the simple process of blindfolded selection from Who's Which.

The motto of this most stately of earthly institutions is a peculiarly modest, truthful, and unintentional epigram by Tupper:

"Unknown, I became Famous; Famous, I remain Unknown."

And so I found it to be the case; for, when at last I was privileged to write my name, "Smith, Academician," I discovered to my surprise that I knew none of my brother Immortals, and, more amazing still, none of them had ever heard of me.

This latter fact became the more astonishing to me as I learned the identity of the other Immortals.

Even the President of our great republic was numbered among these Olympians. I had every right to suppose that he had heard of me. I had happened to hear of him, because his Secretary of State once mentioned him at Chautauqua.

It was a wonderfully meaningless sensation to know nobody and to discover myself equally unknown amid that matchless companionship. We were like a mixed bunch of gods, Greek, Norse, Hindu, Hottentot—all gathered on Olympus, having never heard of each other but taking it for granted that we were all gods together and all members of this club.

My initiation into the Academy had been fixed for April first, and I was much worried concerning the address which I was of course expected to deliver on that occasion before my fellow members.

It had to be an exciting address because slumber was not an infrequent phenomenon among the Immortals on such solemn occasions. Like dozens of dozing Joves a dull discourse always set them nodding.

But always under such circumstances the pretty ushers from Barnard College passed around refreshments; a suffragette orchestra struck up; the ushers uprooted the seated Immortals and fox-trotted them into comparative consciousness.

But I didn't wish to have my inaugural address interrupted, therefore I was at my wits' ends to discover a subject of such exciting scientific interest that my august audience could not choose but listen as attentively as they would listen from the front row to some deathless stunt in vaudeville.

That morning I had left the Bronx rather early, hoping that a long walk might compose my thoughts and enable me to think of some sufficiently entertaining and unusual subject for my inaugural address.

I walked as far as Columbia University, gazed with rapture upon its magnificent architecture until I was as satiated as though I had arisen from a banquet at Childs'.

To aid mental digestion I strolled over to the noble home of the Academy and Institute adjoining Mr. Huntington's Hispano-Moresque Museum.

It was a fine, sunny morning, and the Immortals were being exercised by a number of pretty ushers from Barnard.

I gazed upon the impressive procession with pride unutterable; very soon I also should walk two and two in the sunshine, my dome crowned with figurative laurels, cracking scientific witticisms with my fellow inmates, or, perhaps, squeezing the pretty fingers of some—But let that pass.

I was, as I say, gazing upon this inspiring scene on a beautiful morning in February, when I became aware of a short and visibly vulgar person beside me, plucking persistently at my elbow.

"Are you the great Academician, Perfessor Smith?" he asked, tipping his pearl-coloured and somewhat soiled bowler.

"Yes," I said condescendingly. "Your description of me precludes further doubt. What can I do for you, my good man?"

"Are you this here Perfessor Smith of the Department of Anthropology in the Bronx Park Zoölogical Society?" he persisted.

"What do you desire of me?" I repeated, taking another look at him. He was exceedingly ordinary.

"Prof, old sport," he said cordially, "I took a slant at the papers yesterday, an' I seen all about the big time these guys had when you rode the goat—"

"Rode—what?"

"When you was elected. Get me?"

I stared at him. He grinned in a friendly way.

"The privacy of those solemn proceedings should remain sacred. It were unfit to discuss such matters with the world at large," I said coldly.

"I get you," he rejoined cheerfully.

"What do you desire of me?" I repeated. "Why this unseemly apropos?"

"I was comin' to it. Perfessor, I'll be frank. I need money—"

"You need brains!"

"No," he said good-humouredly, "I've got 'em; plenty of 'em; I'm overstocked with idees. What I want to do is to sell you a few—"

"Do you know you are impudent!"

"Listen, friend. I seen a piece in the papers as how you was to make the speech of your life when you ride the goat for these here guys on April first—"

"I decline to listen—"

"One minute, friend! I want to ask you one thing! What are you going to talk about?"

I was already moving away but I stopped and stared at him.

"That's the question," he nodded with unimpaired cheerfulness, "what are you going to talk about on April the first? Remember it's the hot-air party of your life. Ree-member that each an' every paper in the United States will print what you say. Now, how about it, friend? Are you up in your lines?"

Swallowing my repulsion for him I said: "Why are you concerned as to what may be the subject of my approaching address?"

"There you are, Prof!" he exclaimed delightedly; "I want to do business with you. That's me! I'm frank about it. Say, there ought to be a wad of the joyful in it for us both—"

"What?"

"Sure. We can work it any old way. Take Tyng, Tyng and Company, the typewriter people. I'd be ashamed to tell you what I can get out o' them if you'll mention the Tyng-Tyng typewriter in your speech—"

"What you suggest is infamous!" I said haughtily.

"Believe me there's enough in it to make it a financial coup, and I ask you, Prof, isn't a financial coup respectable?"

"You seem to be morally unfitted to comprehend—"

"Pardon me! I'm fitted up regardless with all kinds of fixtures. I'm fixed to undertake anything. Now if you'd prefer the Bunsen Baby Biscuit bunch—why old man Bunsen would come across—"

"I won't do such things!" I said angrily.

"Very well, very well. Don't get riled, sir. That's only one way to build on Fifth Avenoo. I've got one hundred thousand other ways—"

"I don't want to talk to you—"

"They're honest—some of them. Say, if you want a stric'ly honest deal I've got the goods. Only it ain't as easy and the money ain't as big—"

"I don't want to talk to you—"

"Yes you do. You don't reelize it but you do. Why you're fixin' to make the holler of your life, ain't you? What are you goin' to say? Hey? What you aimin' to say to make those guys set up? What's the use of up-stagin'? Ain't you willin' to pay me a few plunks if I dyvulge to you the most startlin' phenomena that has ever electrified civilization sense the era of P.T. Barnum!"

I was already hurrying away when the mention of that great scientist's name halted me once more.

The little flashy man had been tagging along at my heels, talking cheerfully and volubly all the while; and now, as I halted again, he struck an attitude, legs apart, thumbs hooked in his armpits, and his head cocked knowingly on one side.

"Prof," he said, "if you'd work in the Tyng-Tyng Company, or fix it up with Bunsen to mention his Baby Biscuits as the most nootritious of condeements, there'd be more in it for you an' me. But it's up to you."

"Well I won't!" I retorted.

"Very well, ve-ry well," he said soothingly. "Then look over another line o' samples. No trouble to show 'em—none at all, sir! Now if P.T. Barnum was alive—"

I said very seriously: "The name of that great discoverer falling from your illiterate lips has halted me a second time. His name alone invests your somewhat suspicious conversation with a dignity and authority heretofore conspicuously absent. If, as you hint, you have any scientific information for sale which P.T. Barnum might have considered worth purchasing, you may possibly find in me a client. Proceed, young sir."

"Say, listen, Bo—I mean, Prof. I've got the goods. Don't worry. I've got information in my think-box that would make your kick-in speech the event of the century. The question remains, do I get mine?"

"What is this scientific information?"

We had now walked as far as Riverside Drive. There were plenty of unoccupied benches. I sat down and he seated himself beside me.

For a few moments I gazed upon the magnificent view. Even he seemed awed by the proportions of the superb iron gas tank dominating the prospect.

I gazed at the colossal advertisements across the Hudson, at the freight trains below; I gazed upon the lordly Hudson itself, that majestic sewer which drains the Empire State, bearing within its resistless flood millions of tons of insoluble matter from that magic fairyland which we call "up-state," to the sea. And, thinking of disposal plants, I thought of that sublime paraphrase—"From the Mohawk to the Hudson, and from the Hudson to the Sea."

"Bo," he said, "I gotta hand it to you. Them guys might have got wise if you had worked in the Tyng-Tyng Company or the Bunsen stuff. There was big money into it, but it might not have went."

I waited curiously.

"But this here dope I'm startin' in to cook for you is a straight, reelible, an' hones' pill. P.T. Barnum he would have went a million miles to see what I seen last Janooary down in the Coquina country—"

"Where is that?"

"Say; that's what costs money to know. When I put you wise I'm due to retire from actyve business. Get me?"

"Go on."

"Sure. I was down to the Coquina country, a-doin'—well, I was doin' rubes. I gotta be hones' with you, Prof. That's what I was a-doin' of—sellin' farms under water to suckers. Bee-u-tiful Florida! Own your own orange grove. Seven crops o' strawberries every winter in Gawd's own country—get me?"

He bestowed upon me a loathsome wink.

"Well, it went big till I made a break and got in Dutch with the Navy Department what was surveyin' the Everglades for a safe and sane harbor of refuge for the navy in time o' war.

"Sir, they was a-dredgin' up the farms I was sellin', an' the suckers heard of it an' squealed somethin' fierce, an' I had to hustle! Yes, sir, I had to git up an' mosey cross-lots. And what with the Federal Gov'ment chasin' me one way an' them rubes an' the sheriff of Pickalocka County racin' me t'other, I got lost for fair—yes, sir."

He smiled reminiscently, produced from his pockets the cold and offensive remains of a partly consumed cigar, and examined it critically. Then he requested a match.

"I shall now pass over lightly or in subdood silence the painful events of my flight," he remarked, waving his cigar and expelling a long squirt of smoke from his unshaven lips. "Surfice it to say that I got everythin' that was comin' to me, an' then some, what with snakes and murskeeters, an' briers an' mud, an' hunger an' thirst an' heat. Wasn't there a wop named Pizarro or somethin' what got lost down in Florida? Well, he's got nothin' on me. I never want to see the dam' state again. But I'll go back if you say so!"

His small rat eyes rested musingly upon the river; he sucked thoughtfully at his cigar, hooked one soiled thumb into the armhole of his fancy vest and crossed his legs.

"To resoom," he said cheerily; "I come out one day, half nood, onto the banks of the Miami River. The rest was a pipe after what I had went through.

"I trimmed a guy at Miami, got clothes and railroad fare, an' ducked.

"Now the valyble portion of my discourse is this here partial information concernin' what I seen—or rather what I run onto durin' my crool flight from my ree-lentless persecutors.

"An' these here is the facts: There is, contrary to maps, Coast Survey guys, an' general opinion, a range of hills in Florida, made entirely of coquina.

"It's a good big range, too, fifty miles long an' anywhere from one to five miles acrost.

"An' what I've got to say is this: Into them there Coquina hills there still lives the expirin' remains of the cave-men—"

"What!" I exclaimed incredulously.

"Or," he continued calmly, "to speak more stric'ly, the few individools of that there expirin' race is now totally reduced to a few women."

"Your statement is wild—"

"No; but they're wild. I seen 'em. Bein' extremely bee-utiful I approached nearer, but they hove rocks at me, they did, an' they run into the rocks like squir'ls, they did, an' I was too much on the blink to stick around whistlin' for dearie.

"But I seen 'em; they was all dolled up in the skins of wild annermals. When I see the first one she was eatin' onto a ear of corn, an' I nearly ketched her, but she run like hellnall—yes, sir. Just like that.

"So next I looked for some cave guy to waltz up an' paste me, but no. An' after I had went through them dam' Coquina mountains I realized that there was nary a guy left in this here expirin' race, only women, an' only about a dozen o' them."

He ceased, meditatively expelled a cloud of pungent smoke, and folded his arms.

"Of course," said I with a sneer, "you have proofs to back your pleasant tale?"

"Sure. I made a map."

"I see," said I sarcastically. "You propose to have me pay you for that map?"

"Sure."

"How much, my confiding friend?"

"Ten thousand plunks."

I began to laugh. He laughed, too: "You'll pay 'em if you take my map an' go to the Coquina hills," he said.

I stopped laughing: "Do you mean that I am to go there and investigate before I pay you for this information?"

"Sure. If the goods ain't up to sample the deal is off."

"Sample? What sample?" I demanded derisively.

He made a gesture with one soiled hand as though quieting a balky horse.

"I took a snapshot, friend. You wanta take a slant at it?"

"You took a photograph of one of these alleged cave-dwellers?"

"I took ten but when these here cave-ladies hove rocks at me the fillums was put on the blink—all excep' this one which I dee-veloped an' printed."

He drew from his inner coat pocket a photograph and handed it to me—the most amazing photograph I ever gazed upon. Astounded, almost convinced I sat looking at this irrefutable evidence in silence. The smoke of his cigar drifting into my face aroused me from a sort of dazed inertia.

"Listen," I said, half strangled, "are you willing to wait for payment until I personally have verified the existence of these—er—creatures?"

"You betcher! When you have went there an' have saw the goods, just let me have mine if they're up to sample. Is that right?"

"It seems perfectly fair."

"It is fair. I wouldn't try to do a scientific guy—no, sir. Me without no eddycation, only brains? Fat chance I'd have to put one over on a Academy sport what's chuck-a-block with Latin an' Greek an' scientific stuff an' all like that!"

I admitted to myself that he'd stand no chance.

"Is it a go?" he asked.

"Where is the map?" I inquired, trembling internally with excitement.

"Ha—ha!" he said. "Listen to my mirth! The map is inside here, old sport!" and he tapped his retreating forehead with one nicotine-stained finger.

"I see," said I, trying to speak carelessly; "you desire to pilot me."

"I don't desire to but I gotta go with you."

"An accurate map—"

"Can it, old sport! A accurate map is all right when it's pasted over the front of your head for a face. But I wear the other kind of map inside me conk. Get me?"

"I confess that I do not."

"Well, get this, then. It's a cash deal. If the goods is up to sample you hand me mine then an' there. I don't deliver no goods f.o.b. I shows 'em to you. After you have saw them it's up to you to round 'em up. That's all, as they say when our great President pulls a gun. There ain't goin' to be no shootin'; walk out quietly, ladies!"

After I had sat there for fully ten minutes staring at him I came to the only logical conclusion possible to a scientific mind.

I said: "You are, admittedly, unlettered; you are confessedly a chevalier of industry; personally you are exceedingly distasteful to me. But it is useless to deny that you are the most extraordinary man I ever saw.... How soon can you take me to these Coquina hills?"

"Gimme twenty-four hours to—fix things," he said gaily.

"Is that all?"

"It's plenty, I guess. An'—say!"

"What?"

"It's a stric'ly cash deal. Get me?"

"I shall have with me a certified check for ten thousand dollars. Also a pair of automatics."

He laughed: "Huh!" he said, "I could loco your cabbage-palm soup if I was that kind! I'm on the level, Perfessor. If I wasn't I could get you in about a hundred styles while you was blinkin' at what you was a-thinkin' about. But I ain't no gun-man. You hadn't oughta pull that stuff on me. I've give you your chanst; take it or leave it."

I pondered profoundly for another ten minutes. And at last my decision was irrevocably reached.

"It's a bargain," I said firmly. "What is your name?"

"Sam Mink. Write it Samuel onto that there certyfied check—if you can spare the extra seconds from your valooble time."

II

On Monday, the first day of March, 1915, about 10:30 a.m., we came in sight of something which, until I had met Mink, I never had dreamed existed in southern Florida—a high range of hills.

It had been an eventless journey from New York to Miami, from Miami to Fort Coquina; but from there through an absolutely pathless wilderness as far as I could make out, the journey had been exasperating.

Where we went I do not know even now: saw-grass and water, hammock and shell mound, palm forests, swamps, wildernesses of water-oak and live-oak, vast stretches of pine, lagoons, sloughs, branches, muddy creeks, reedy reaches from which wild fowl rose in clouds where alligators lurked or lumbered about after stranded fish, horrible mangrove thickets full of moccasins and water-turkeys, heronry more horrible still, out of which the heat from a vertical sun distilled the last atom of nauseating effluvia—all these choice spots we visited under the guidance of the wretched Mink. I seemed to be missing nothing that might discourage or disgust me.

He appeared to know the way, somehow, although my compass became mysteriously lost the first day out from Fort Coquina.

Again and again I felt instinctively that we were travelling in a vast circle, but Mink always denied it, and I had no scientific instruments to verify my deepening suspicions.

Another thing bothered me: Mink did not seem to suffer from insects or heat; in fact, to my intense annoyance, he appeared to be having a comfortable time of it, eating and drinking with gusto, sleeping snugly under a mosquito bar, permitting me to do all camp work, the paddling as long as we used a canoe, and all the cooking, too, claiming, on his part, a complete ignorance of culinary art.

Sometimes he condescended to catch a few fish for the common pan; sometimes he bestirred himself to shoot a duck or two. But usually he played on his concertina during his leisure moments which were plentiful.

I began to detest Samuel Mink.

At first I was murderously suspicious of him, and I walked about with my automatic arsenal ostentatiously displayed. But he looked like such a miserable little shrimp that I became ashamed of my precautions. Besides, as he cheerfully pointed out, a little koonti soaked in my drinking water, would have done my business for me if he had meant me any physical harm. Also he had a horrid habit of noosing moccasins for sport; and it would have been easy for him to introduce one to me while I slept.

Really what most worried me was the feeling which I could not throw off that somehow or other we were making very little progress in any particular direction.

He even admitted that there was reason for my doubts, but he confided to me that to find these Coquina hills, was like traversing a maze. Doubling to and fro among forests and swamps, he insisted, was the only possible path of access to the undiscovered Coquina hills of Florida. Otherwise, he argued, these Coquina hills would long ago have been discovered.

And it seemed to me that he had been right when at last we came out on the edge of a palm forest and beheld that astounding blue outline of hills in a country which has always been supposed to lie as flat as a flabby flap-jack.

A desert of saw-palmetto stretched away before us to the base of the hills; game trails ran through it in every direction like sheep paths; a few moth-eaten Florida deer trotted away as we appeared.

Into one of these trails stepped Samuel Mink, burdened only with his concertina and a box of cigars. I, loaded with seventy pounds of impedimenta including a moving-picture apparatus, reeled after him.

He walked on jauntily toward the hills, his pearl-coloured bowler hat at an angle. Occasionally he played upon his concertina as he advanced; now and then he cut a pigeon wing. I hated him. At every toilsome step I hated him more deeply. He played "Tipperary" on his concertina.

"See 'em, old top?" he inquired, nodding toward the hills. "I'm a man of my word, I am. Look at 'em! Take 'em in, old sport! An' reemember, each an' every hill is guaranteed to contain one bony fidy cave-lady what is the last vanishin' traces of a extinc' an' dissappeerin' race!"

We toiled on—that is, I did, bowed under my sweating load of paraphernalia. He skipped in advance like some degenerate twentieth century faun, playing on his pipes the unmitigated melodies of George Cohan.

"Watch your step!" he cried, nimbly avoiding the attentions of a ground-rattler which tried to caress his ankle from under a saw-palmetto.

With a shudder I gave the deadly little reptile room and floundered forward a prey to exhaustion, melancholy, and red-bugs. A few buzzards kept pace with me, their broad, black shadows gliding ominously over the sun-drenched earth; blue-tail lizards went rustling and leaping away on every side; floppy soft-winged butterflies escorted me; a strange bird which seemed to be dressed in a union suit of checked gingham, flew from tree to tree as I plodded on, and squealed at me persistently.

At last I felt the hard coquina under foot; the cool blue shadow of the hills enveloped me; I slipped off my pack, dumped it beside a little rill of crystal water which ran sparkling from the hills, and sat down on a soft and fragrant carpet of hound's-tongue.

After a while I drank my fill at the rill, bathed head, neck, face and arms, and, feeling delightfully refreshed, leaned back against the fern-covered slab of coquina.

"What are you doing?" I demanded of Mink who was unpacking the kit and disengaging the moving-picture machine.

"Gettin' ready," he replied, fussing busily with the camera.

"You don't expect to see any cave people here, do you?" I asked with a thrill of reviving excitement.

"Why not?"

"Here?"

"Cert'nly. Why the first one I seen was a-drinkin' into this brook."

"Here! Where I'm sitting?" I asked incredulously.

"Yes, sir, right there. It was this way; I was lyin' down, tryin' to figure the shortes' way to Fort Coquina, an' wishin' I was nearer Broadway than I was to the Equator, when I heard a voice say, 'Blub-blub, muck-a-muck!' an' then I seen two cave-ladies come sof'ly stealin' along."

"W-where?"

"Right there where you are a-sittin'. Say, they was lookers! An' they come along quiet like two big-eyed deer, kinder nosin' the air and listenin'.

"'Gee whiz,' thinks I, 'Longacre ain't got so much on them dames!' An' at that one o' them wore a wild-cat's skin an' that's all—an' a wild-cat ain't big. And t'other she sported pa'm-leaf pyjamas.

"So when they don't see nothin' around to hinder, they just lays down flat and takes a drink into that pool, lookin' up every swallow like little birds listenin' and kinder thankin' God for a good square drink.

"I knowed they was wild girls soon as I seen 'em. Also they sez to one another, 'Blub-blub!' Kinder sof'ly. All the same I've seen wilder ladies on Broadway so I took a chanst where I was squattin' behind a rock.

"So sez I, 'Ah there, sweetie Blub-blub! Have a taxi on me!' An' with that they is on their feet, quiverin' all over an' nosin' the wind. So first I took some snapshots at 'em with my Bijoo camera.

"I guess they scented me all right for I seen their eyes grow bigger, an' then they give a bound an' was off over the rocks; an' me after 'em. Say, that was some steeple-chase until a few more cave-ladies come out on them rocks above us an' hove chunks of coquina at me.

"An' with all that dodgin' an' duckin' of them there rocks the cave-girls got away; an' I seen 'em an' the other cave-ladies scurryin' into little caves—one whisked into this hole, another scuttled into that—bing! all over!

"All I could think of was to light a cigar an' blow the smoke in after the best-lookin' cave-girl. But I couldn't smoke her out, an' I hadn't time to starve her out. So that's all I know about this here pree-historic an' extinc' race o' vanishin' cave-ladies."

As his simple and illiterate narrative advanced I became proportionally excited; and, when he ended, I sprang to my feet in an uncontrollable access of scientific enthusiasm:

"Was she really pretty?" I asked.

"Listen, she was that peachy—"

"Enough!" I cried. "Science expects every man to do his duty! Are your films ready to record a scene without precedent in the scientific annals of creation?"

"They sure is!"

"Then place your camera and your person in a strategic position. This is a magnificent spot for an ambush! Come over beside me!"

He came across to where I had taken cover among the ferns behind the parapet of coquina, and with a thrill of pardonable joy I watched him unlimber his photographic artillery and place it in battery where my every posture and action would be recorded for posterity if a cave-lady came down to the water-hole to drink.

"It were futile," I explained to him in a guarded voice, "for me to attempt to cajole her as you attempted it. Neither playful nor moral suasion could avail, for it is certain that no cave-lady understands English."

"I thought o' that, too," he remarked. "I said, 'Blub-blub! muck-a-muck!' to 'em when they started to run, but it didn't do no good."

I smiled: "Doubtless," said I, "the spoken language of the cave-dweller is made up of similarly primitive exclamations, and you were quite right in attempting to communicate with the cave-ladies and establish a cordial entente. Professor Garner has done so among the Simian population of Gaboon. Your attempt is most creditable and I shall make it part of my record.

"But the main idea is to capture a living specimen of cave-lady, and corroborate every detail of that pursuit and capture upon the films.

"And believe me, Mr. Mink," I added, my voice trembling with emotion, "no Academician is likely to go to sleep when I illustrate my address with such pictures as you are now about to take!"

"The police might pull the show," he suggested.

"No," said I, "Science is already immune; art is becoming so. Only nature need fear the violence of prejudice; and doubtless she will continue to wear pantalettes and common-sense nighties as long as our great republic endures."

I unslung my field-glasses, adjusted them and took a penetrating squint at the hillside above.

Nothing stirred up there except a buzzard or two wheeling on tip-curled pinions above the palms.

Presently Mink inquired whether I had "lamped" anything, and I replied that I had not.

"They may be snoozin' in their caves," he suggested. "But don't you fret, old top; you'll get what's comin' to you and I'll get mine."

"About that check—" I began and hesitated.

"Sure. What about it?"

"I suppose I'm to give it to you when the first cave-woman appears."

"That's what!"

I pondered the matter for a while in silence. I could see no risk in paying him this draft on sight.

"All right," I said. "Bring on your cave-dwellers."

Hour succeeded hour, but no cave-dwellers came down to the pool to drink. We ate luncheon—a bit of cold duck, some koonti-bread, and a dish of palm-cabbage. I smoked an inexpensive cigar; Mink lit a more pretentious one. Afterward he played on his concertina at my suggestion on the chance that the music might lure a cave-girl down the hill. Nymphs were sometimes caught that way, and modern science seems to be reverting more and more closely to the simpler truths of the classics which, in our ignorance and arrogance, we once dismissed as fables unworthy of scientific notice.

However this Broadway faun piped in vain: no white-footed dryad came stealing through the ferns to gaze, perhaps to dance to the concertina's plaintive melodies.

So after a while he put his concertina into his pocket, cocked his derby hat on one side, gathered his little bandy legs under his person, and squatted there in silence, chewing the wet and bitter end of his extinct cigar.

Toward mid-afternoon I unslung my field-glasses again and surveyed the hill.

At first I noticed nothing, not even a buzzard; then, of a sudden, my attention was attracted to something moving among the fern-covered slabs of coquina just above where we lay concealed—a slim, graceful shape half shadowed under a veil of lustrous hair which glittered like gold in the sun.

"Mink!" I whispered hoarsely. "One of them is coming! This—

this indeed is the stupendous and crowning climax of my scientific career!"

His comment was incredibly coarse: "Gimme the dough," he said without a tremor of surprise. Indeed there was a metallic ring of menace in his low and entirely cold tones as he laid one hand on my arm. "No welchin'," he said, "or I put the whole show on the bum!"

The overwhelming excitement of the approaching crisis neutralized my disgust; I fished out the certified check from my pocket and flung the miserable scrap of paper at him. "Get your machine ready!" I hissed. "Do you understand what these moments mean to the civilized world!"

"I sure do," he said.

Nearer and nearer came the lithe white figure under its glorious crown of hair, moving warily and gracefully amid the great coquina slabs—nearer, nearer, until I no longer required my glasses.

She was a slender red-lipped thing, blue-eyed, dainty of hand and foot.

The spotted pelt of a wild-cat covered her, or attempted to.

I unfolded a large canvas sack as she approached the pool. For a moment or two she stood gazing around her and her close-set ears seemed to be listening. Then, apparently satisfied, she threw back her beautiful young head and sent a sweet wild call floating back to the sunny hillside.

"Blub-blub!" rang her silvery voice; "blub-blub! Muck-a-muck!" And from the fern-covered hollows above other voices replied joyously to her reassuring call, "Blub-blub-blub!"

The whole bunch was coming down to drink—the entire remnant of a prehistoric and almost extinct race of human creatures was coming to quench its thirst at this water-hole. How I wished for James Barnes at the camera's crank! He alone could do justice to this golden girl before me.

One by one, clad in their simple yet modest gowns of pelts and garlands, five exquisitely superb specimens of cave-girl came gracefully down to the water-hole to drink.

Almost swooning with scientific excitement I whispered to the unspeakable Mink: "Begin to crank as soon as I move!" And, gathering up my big canvas sack I rose, and, still crouching, stole through the ferns on tip-toe.

They had already begun to drink when they heard me; I must have made some slight sound in the ferns, for their keen ears detected it and they sprang to their feet.

It was a magnificent sight to see them there by the pool, tense, motionless, at gaze, their dainty noses to the wind, their beautiful eyes wide and alert.

For a moment, enchanted, I remained spellbound in the presence of this prehistoric spectacle, then, waving my sack, I sprang out from behind the rock and cantered toward them.

Instead of scattering and flying up the hillside they seemed paralyzed, huddling together as though to get into the picture. Delighted I turned and glanced at Mink; he was cranking furiously.

With an uncontrollable shout of triumph and delight I pranced toward the huddling cave-girls, arms outspread as though heading a horse or concentrating chickens. And, totally forgetting the uselessness of urbanity and civilized speech as I danced around that lovely but terrified group, "Ladies!" I cried, "do not be alarmed, because I mean only kindness and proper respect. Civilization calls you from the wilds! Sentiment, pity, piety propel my legs, not the ruthless desire to injure or enslave you! Ladies! You are under the wing of science. An anthropologist is speaking to you! Fear nothing! Rather rejoice! Your wonderful race shall be rescued from extinction—even if I have to do it myself! Ladies, don't run!" They had suddenly scattered and were now beginning to dodge me. "I come among you bearing the precious promises of education, of religion, of equal franchise, of fashion!"

"Blub-blub!" they whimpered continuing to dodge me.

"Yes!" I cried in an excess of transcendental enthusiasm. "Blub-blub! And though I do not comprehend the exquisite simplicity of your primeval speech, I answer with all my heart, 'Blub-blub!'"

Meanwhile, they were dodging and eluding me as I chased first one, then another, one hand outstretched, the other invitingly clutching the sack.

A hasty glance at Mink now and then revealed him industriously cranking away.

Once I fell into the pool. That section of the film should never be released, I determined, as I blew the water out of my mouth, gasped, and started after a lovely, ruddy-haired cave-girl whose curiosity had led her to linger beside the pool in which I was floundering.

But run as fast as I could and skip hither and thither with all the agility I could muster I did not seem to be able to seize a single cave-girl.

Every few minutes, baffled and breathless, I rested; and they always clustered together uttering their plaintively musical "blub-blub," not apparently very much afraid of me, and even exhibiting curiosity. Now and then they cast glances toward Mink who was grinding away steadily, and I could scarcely retain a shout of joy as I realized what wonderful pictures he was taking. Indeed luck seemed to be with me, so far, for never once did these beautiful prehistoric creatures retire out of photographic range.

But otherwise the problem was becoming serious. I could not catch one of them; they eluded me with maddening swiftness and grace; my pauses to recover my breath became more frequent.

At last, dead beat, I sat down on a slab of coquina. And when I was able to articulate I turned around toward Mink.

"You'll have to drop your camera and come over and help me," I panted. "I'm all in!"

"Not quite," he said.

For a moment I did not understand him; then under my outraged eyes, and within the hearing of my horrified ears a terrible thing occurred.

"Now, ladies!" yelled Mink, "all on for the fine-ally! Up-stage there, you red-headed little spot-crabber! Mabel! Take the call! Now smile the whole bloomin' bunch of you!"

What was he saying? I did not comprehend. I stared dully at the six cave-girls as they grouped themselves in a semi-circle behind me.

Then, as one of them came up and unfolded a white strip of cloth behind my head, the others drew from concealed pockets in their kilts of cat-fur, little silk flags of all nations and began to wave them.

Paralyzed I turned my head. On the strip of white cloth, which the tallest cave-girl was holding directly behind my head, was printed in large black letters:

SUNSET SOAP

For one cataclysmic instant I gazed upon this hideous spectacle, then with an unearthly cry I collapsed into the arms of the nicest looking one.

There is little more to say. Contrary to my fears the release of this outrageous film did not injure my scientific standing. Modern science, accustomed to proprietary testimonials, has become reconciled to such things.

My appearance upon the films in the movies in behalf of Sunset Soap, oddly enough, seemed to enhance my scientific reputation. Even such austere purists as Guilford, the Cubist poet, congratulated me upon my fearless independence of ethical tradition.

And I had lived to learn a gentler truth than that, for, the pretty girl who had been cast for Cave-girl No. 3—But let that pass. Adhibenda est in jocando moderatio.

Sweet are the uses of advertisement.

THE LADIES OF THE LAKE

I

At the suggestion of several hundred thousand ladies desiring to revel and possibly riot in the saturnalia of equal franchise, the unnamed lakes in that vast and little known region in Alaska bounded by the Ylanqui River and the Thunder Mountains were now being inexorably named after women.

It was a beautiful thought. Already several exquisite, lonely bits of water, gem-set among the eternal peaks, mirrors for cloud and soaring eagle, a glass for the moon as keystone to the towering arch of stars, had been irrevocably labelled.

Already there was Lake Amelia Jones, Lake Sadie Dingleheimer, Lake Maggie McFadden, and Lake Mrs. Gladys Doolittle Batt.

I longed to see these lakes under the glamour of their newly added beauty.

Imagine, therefore, my surprise and happiness when I received the following communication from my revered and beloved chief, Professor Farrago, dated from the Smithsonian Institute, Washington, whither he had been summoned in haste to examine and pronounce upon the identity of a very small bird supposed to be a specimen of that rare and almost extinct creature, the two-toed titmouse, Mustitta duototus, to be scientifically exact, as I invariably strive to be.

The important letter in question was as follows:

To Percy Smith, B.S., D.F., etc., etc., Curator, Department of Anthropology, Administration Building, Bronx Park, N.Y.

My Dear Mr. Smith:

Several very important and determined ladies, recently honoured by the Government in having a number of lakes in Alaska named after them, have decided to make a pilgrimage to that region, inspired by a characteristic desire to gaze upon the lakes named after them individually.

They request information upon the following points:

1st. Are the waters of the lakes in that locality sufficiently clear for a lady to do her hair by? In that event, the expedition will not burden itself with looking-glasses.

2nd. Are there any hotels? (You need merely say, no. I have tried to explain to them that it is, for the most part, an unexplored wilderness, but they insist upon further information from you.)

3rd. If there are hotels, is there also running water to be had? (You may tell them that there is plenty of running water.)

4th. What are the summer outdoor amusements? (You may inform them that there is plenty of bathing, boating, fishing, and an abundance of shade trees. Also, excellent mountain-climbing to be had in the vicinity. You need not mention the pastimes of "Hunt the Flea" or "Dodge the Skeeter.")

I am not by nature cruel, Mr. Smith, but when these ladies informed me that they had decided to penetrate that howling and unexplored wilderness without being burdened or interfered with by any member of my sex, for one horrid and criminal moment I hoped they would. Because in that event none of them would ever come back.

However, in my heart milder and more humane sentiments prevailed. I pointed out to them the peril of their undertaking, the dangers of an unexplored region, the necessity of masculine guidance and support.

My earnestness and solicitude were, I admit, prompted partly by a desire to utilize this expensively projected expedition as a vehicle for the accumulation of scientific data.

As soon as I heard of it I conceived the plan of attaching two members of our Bronx Park scientific staff to the expedition—you, and Mr. Brown.

But no sooner did these determined ladies hear of it than they repelled the suggestion with indignation.

Now, the matter stands as follows: These ladies don't want any man in the expedition; but they have at last realized that they've got to take a guide or two. And there are no feminine guides in Alaska.

Therefore, considering the immense and vital importance of such an opportunity to explore and report upon this unknown region at somebody else's expense, I suggest that you and Brown meet these ladies at Lake Mrs. Susan W. Pillsbury, which lies on the edge of the region to be explored; that you, without actually perjuring yourselves too horribly, convey to them the misleading impression that you are the promised guides provided for them by a cowed and avuncular Government; and that you take these fearsome ladies about and let them gaze at their reflections in the various lakes named after them; and that, while the expedition lasts, you secretly make such observations, notes, reports, and collections of the flora and fauna of the region as your opportunities may permit.

No time is to be lost. If, at Lake Susan W. Pillsbury, you find regular guides awaiting these ladies, you will bribe these guides to go away and you yourselves will then impersonate the guides. I know of no other way for you to explore this region, as all our available resources at Bronx Park have already been spent in painting appropriate scenery to line the cages of the mammalia, and also in the present exceedingly expensive expedition in search of the polka-dotted boom-bock, which is supposed to inhabit the jungle beyond Lake Niggerplug.

My most solemn and sincere wishes accompany you. Bless you!

Farrago.

II

This, then, is how it came about that "Kitten" Brown and I were seated, one midgeful morning in July, by the pellucid waters of Lake Susan W. Pillsbury, gnawing sections from a greasily fried trout, upon which I had attempted culinary operations.

Brown's baptismal name was William; but the unfortunate young man was once discovered indiscreetly embracing a pretty assistant in the Administration Building at Bronx, and, furthermore, was overheard to address her as "Kitten."

So Kitten Brown it was for him in future. After he had fought all the younger members of the scientific staff in turn, he gradually became resigned to this annoying nom d'amour.

Lightly but thoroughly equipped for scientific field research, we had arrived at the rendezvous in time to bribe the two guides engaged by the Government to go back to their own firesides.

A week later the formidable expedition of representative ladies arrived; and now they were sitting on the shore of Lake Susan W. Pillsbury, at a little distance from us, trying to keep the midges from their features and attempting to eat the fare provided for them by me.

I myself couldn't eat it. No wonder they murmured. But hunger goaded them to attack the greasy mess of trout and fried cornmeal.

Kitten was saying to me:

"Our medicine chest isn't very extensive. I hope they brought their own. If they didn't, some among us will never again see New York."

I stole a furtive glance at the unfortunate women. There was one among them—but let me first enumerate their heavy artillery:

There was the Reverend Dr. Amelia Jones, blond, adipose, and close to the four-score mark. She stepped high in the Equal Franchise ranks. Nobody had ever had the temerity to answer her back.

There was Miss Sadie Dingleheimer, fifty, emaciated, anemic, and gauntly glittering with thick-lensed eye-glasses. She was the President of the National Prophylactic Club, whatever that may be.

There was Miss Margaret McFadden, a Titian, profusely toothed, muscular, and President of the Hair Dressers' Union of the United States.

There was Mrs. Gladys Doolittle Batt, a grass one—Batt being represented as a vanishing point—President of the National Eugenic and Purity League; tall, gnarled, sinuously powerful, and prone to emotional attacks. The attacks were directed toward others.

These, then, composed the heavy artillery. The artillery of the light brigade consisted only of a single piece. Her name was Angelica White, a delegate from the Trained Nurses' Association of America. The nurses had been too busy with their business to attend such picnics, so one had been selected by lot to represent the busy Association on this expedition.

Angelica White was a tall, fair, yellow-haired girl of twenty-two or three, with violet-blue eyes and red lips, and a way of smiling a little when spoken to—but let that pass. I mean only to be scientifically minute. A passion for fact has ever obsessed me. I have little literary ability and less desire to sully my pen with that degraded form of letters known as fiction. Once in my life my mania for accuracy involved me lyrically. It was a short poem, but an earnest one:

> Truth is mighty and must prevail,
> Otherwise it were inadvisable to tell the tale.

I bestowed it upon the New York Evening Post, but declined remuneration. My message belonged to the world. I don't mean the newspaper.

Her eyes, then, were tinted with that indefinable and agreeable nuance which modifies blue to a lilac or violet hue.

Watching her askance, I was deeply sorry that my cooking seemed to pain her.

"Guide!" said Mrs. Doolittle Batt, in that remarkable, booming voice of hers.

"Ma'am!" said Kitten Brown and I with spontaneous alacrity, leaping from the ground as though shot at.

"This cooking," she said, with an ominous stare at us, "is atrocious. Don't you know how to cook?"

I said with a smiling attempt at ease:

"There are various ways of cooking food for the several species of mammalia which an all-wise Providence—"

"Do you think you're cooking for wild-cats?" she demanded.

Our smiles faded.

"It's my opinion that you're incompetent," remarked the Reverend Dr. Jones, slapping at midges with a hand that might have rocked all the cradles of the nation, but had not rocked any.

"We're not getting our money's worth," said Miss Dingleheimer, "even if the Government does pay your salaries."

I looked appealingly from one stony face to another. In Miss McFadden's eye there was the somber glint of battle. She said:

"If you can guide us no better than you cook, God save us all this day week!" And she hurled the contents of her tin plate into Lake Susan W. Pillsbury.

Mrs. Doolittle Batt arose:

"Come," she said; "it is time we started. What is the name of the first lake we may hope to encounter?"

We knew no more than did they, but we said that Lake Gladys Doolittle Batt was the first, hoping to placate that fearsome woman.

"Come on, then!" she cried, picking up her carved and varnished mountain staff.

Miss Dingleheimer had brought one, too, from the Catskills.

So Kitten Brown and I loaded our mule, set him in motion, and drove him forward into the unknown.

Where we were going we had not the slightest idea; the margin of the lake was easy travelling, so easy that we never noticed that we had already gone around the lake three times, until Mrs. Batt recognized the fact and turned on us furiously.

I didn't know how to explain it, except to say feebly that I was doing it as a sort of preliminary canter to harden and inure the ladies.

"We don't need hardening!" she snarled. "Do you understand that!"

I comprehended that at once. But I forced a sickly smile and skipped forward in the wake of my mule, with something of the same abandon which characterizes the flight of an unwelcome dog.

In the terrified ear of Kitten I voiced my doubts concerning the prospects of a pleasant journey.

We marched in the following order: Arthur, the heavily laden mule, led; then came Kitten Brown and myself, all hung over with stew-pans, shotguns, rifles, cartridge-belts, ponchos, and the toilet reticules of the ladies; then marched the Reverend Dr. Jones, and, in order, filing behind her, Miss Dingleheimer, Mrs. Batt, Miss McFadden, and Miss White—the latter in her trained nurse's costume and wearing a red cross on her sleeve—an idea of Mrs. Batt, who believed in emergency methods.

Mrs. Batt also bore a banner, much interfered with by the foliage, bearing the inscription:

EQUAL RIGHTS!
EUGENICS OR EXTERMINATION!

After a while she shouted:

"Guide! Here, you may carry this banner for a while! I'm tired."

Kitten and I took turns with it after that. It was hard work, particularly as one by one in turn they came up and hung their parasols and shopping reticules all over us. We plodded forward like a pair of moving department stores, not daring to shift our burdens to Arthur, because we had already stuffed into the panniers of that simple and dignified animal all our collecting boxes, cyanide jars, butterfly nets, note-books, reels of piano wire, thermometers, barometers, hydrometers, stereometers, aeronoids, adnoids— everything, in fact, that guides are not supposed to pack into the woods, but which we had smuggled unbeknown to those misguided ones we guided.

And, to make room for our scientific paraphernalia, we had been obliged to do a thing so mean, so inexpressibly low, that I blush to relate it. But facts are facts; we discarded nearly a ton of feminine impedimenta. There was fancy work of all sorts in the making or in the raw—materials for knitting, embroidering, tatting, sewing, hemming, stitching, drawn-work, lace-making, crocheting.

Also we disposed of almost half a ton of toilet necessities— powder, perfumery, cosmetics, hot-water bags, slippers, negligees, novels, magazines, bon-bons, chewing-gum, hat-boxes, gloves, stockings, underwear.

We left enough apparel for each lady to change once. They'd have to do some scrubbing now. Science can not be halted by hatpins; cosmos can not be side-tracked by cosmetics.

Toward sunset we came upon a small, crystal clear pond, set between the bases of several lofty mountains. I was ready to drop

45

with fatigue, but I nerved myself, drew a deep, exultant breath, and with one of those fine, sweeping gestures, I cried:

"Lake Mrs. Gladys Doolittle Batt! Eureka! At last! Excelsior!"

There was a profound silence behind me. I turned, striving to mask my apprehension with a smile. The ladies were regarding the pond in surprise. I admit that it was a pond, not a lake.

Injecting into my voice the last remnants of glee which I could summon, I shouted, "Eureka!" and began to caper about as though the size and beauty of the pond had affected me with irrepressible enthusiasm, hoping by my emotion to stampede the convention.

The cold voice of Mrs. Doolittle Batt checked my transports:

"Is that puddle named after me?" she demanded.

"M-ma'am?" I stammered.

"If that wretched frog-pond has been christened with my name, somebody is going to get into trouble," she said ominously.

A profound silence ensued. Arthur patiently switched at flies. As for me, I looked up at the majestic pines, gazed upon the lofty and eternal hills, then ventured a sneaking glance all around me. But I could discover no avenue of escape in case Mrs. Batt should charge me.

"I had been informed," she began dangerously, "that the majestic body of water, which I understood had been honoured with my name, was twelve miles long and three miles wide. This appears to be a puddle!"

"B-b-but it's very p-pretty," I protested feebly. "It's quite round and clear, and it's nearly a quarter of a mile in d-diameter—"

"Mind your business!" retorted Mrs. Doolittle Batt. "I've been swindled!"

Kitten Brown knew more about women than did I. He said in a fairly steady voice:

"Madame, it is an outrage! The women of this mighty nation should make the Government answerable for its duplicity! Your lake should have been at least twenty miles long!"

Everybody turned and looked at Kitten. He was a handsome dog.

"This young man appears to have some trace of common-sense," said Mrs. Batt. "I shall see to it that the Government is held responsible for this odious act of insulting duplicity. I—I won't have my name given to this—this wallow!—" She advanced toward me, her small eyes blazing: I retreated to leeward of Arthur.

"Guide!" she said in a voice still trembling with passion. "Are you certain that you have made no mistake? You appear to be unusually ignorant."

"I am afraid there can be no room for doubt," I said, almost scared out of my senses.

"And on top of this outrage, am I to eat your cooking?" she demanded passionately. "Did I come here to look at this frog-pond and choke on your cooking? Did I?"

"I can cook," said a clear, pleasant voice at my elbow. And Miss White came forward, cool, clean, fresh as a posy in her uniform and cap. I immediately got behind her.

"I can cook very nicely," she said smilingly. "It is part of my profession, you know. So if you two guides will be kind enough to build the fire and help me—" She let her violet eyes linger on me for an instant, then on Brown. A moment later he and I were jostling each other in our eagerness to obey her slightest suggestion. It is that way with men.

So we built her a fire and unpacked our provisions, and we waited very politely on the ladies when dinner was ready.

It was a fine dinner—coffee, bacon, flap-jacks, soup, ash-bread, stewed chicken.

The heavy artillery, made ravenous by their journey, required vast quantities of ammunition. They banqueted largely. I gazed in amazement at Mrs. Doolittle Batt as she swallowed one flap-jack after another, while her eyes bulged larger and larger.

Nor was the capacity of Miss Dingleheimer and the Reverend Dr. Jones to be mocked at by pachyderms.

Brown and I left them eating while we erected the row of little tents. Every lady had demanded a separate tent.

So we cut saplings, set up the silk, drove pegs, and brought armfuls of balsam boughs.

I was afraid they'd demand their knitting and other utensils, but they had eaten to repletion, and were sleepy; and as each toilet case or reticule contained also a nightgown, they drew the flaps of their several tents without insisting that we unpack Arthur's panniers.

They all had disappeared within their tents except Miss White, who insisted on cooking something for us, although we protested that the scraps of the banquet were all right for mere guides.

She stood beside us for a few minutes, watching us busy with our delicious dinner.

"You poor fellows," she said gently. "You are nearly starved."

It is agreeable to be sympathized with by a tall, fair, fresh young girl. We looked up, simpering gratefully.

"This is really a most lovely little lake," she said, gazing out across the still, crystalline water which was all rose and gold in the sunset, save where the sombre shapes of the towering mountains were mirrored in glassy depths.

"It's odd," I said, "that no trout are jumping. There ought to be lots of them there, and this is their jumping hour."

We all looked at the quiet, oval bit of water. Not a circle, not the slightest ripple disturbed it.

"It must be deep," remarked Brown.

We gazed up at the three lofty peaks, the bases of which were the shores of this tiny gem among lakes. Deep, deep, plunging down into dusky profundity, the rocks fell away sheer into limpid depths.

"That little lake may be a thousand feet deep," I said. "In 1903 Professor Farrago, of Bronx Park, measured a lake in the Thunder Mountains, which was two thousand seven hundred and sixty-nine feet deep."

Miss White looked at me curiously.

Into a patch of late sunshine flitted a small butterfly—one of the Grapta species. It settled on a chip of wood, uncoiled its delicate proboscis, and spread its fulvous and deeply indented wings.

"Grapta California," remarked Brown to me.

"Vanessa asteriska" I corrected him. "Note the anal angle of the secondaries and the argentiferous discal area bordering the subcostal nervule."

"The characteristic stripes on the primaries are wanting," he demurred.

"It is double brooded. The summer form lacks the three darker bands."

A few moments' silence was broken by the voice of Miss White.

"I had no idea," she remarked, "that Alaskan guides were so familiar with entomological terms and nomenclature."

We both turned very red.

Brown mumbled something about having picked up a smattering. I added that Brown had taught me.

Perhaps she believed us; her blue eyes rested on us curiously, musingly. Also, at moments, I fancied there was the faintest glint of amusement in them.

She said:

"Two scientific gentlemen from New York requested permission to join this expedition, but Mrs. Batt refused them." She gazed thoughtfully upon the waters of Lake Gladys Doolittle Batt. "I wonder," she murmured, "what became of those two gentlemen."

It was evident that we had betrayed ourselves to this young girl.

She glanced at us again, and perhaps she noticed in our fascinated gaze an expression akin to terror, for suddenly she laughed—such a clear, sweet, silvery little laugh!

"For my part," she said, "I wish they had come with us. I like—
men."

With that she bade us goodnight very politely and went off to
her tent, leaving us with our hats pressed against our stomachs,
attempting by the profundity of our bows to indicate the depth of
our gratitude.

"There's a girl!" exclaimed Brown, as soon as she had
disappeared behind her tent flaps. "She'll never let on to Medusa,
Xantippe, Cassandra and Company. I like that girl, Smith."

"You're not the only one imbued by such sentiments," said I.

He smiled a fatuous and reminiscent smile. He certainly was
good-looking. Presently he said:

"She has the most delightful way of gazing at a man—"

"I've noticed," I said pleasantly.

"Oh. Did she happen to glance at you that way?" he inquired. I
wanted to beat him.

All I said was:

"She's certainly some kitten." Which bottled that young man for
a while.

We lay on the bank of the tiny lake, our backs against a huge
pine-tree, watching the last traces of colour fading from peak and
tree-top.

"Isn't it queer," I said, "that not a trout has splashed? It can't be
that there are no fish in the lake."

"There are such lakes."

"Yes, very deep ones. I wonder how deep this is."

"We'll be out at sunrise with our reel of piano wire and take
soundings," he said. "The heavy artillery won't wake until they're
ready to be loaded with flap-jacks."

I shuddered:

"They're fearsome creatures, Brown. Somehow, that resolute
and bony one has inspired me with a terror unutterable."

"Mrs. Batt?"

"Yes."

He said seriously:

"She'll make a horrid outcry when she asks for her knitting.
What are you going to tell her?"

"I shall say that Indians ambuscaded us while she was asleep,
and carried off all those things."

"You lie very nicely, don't you?" he remarked admiringly.

"In vitium ducit culpæ fuga," said I. "Besides, they don't really
need those articles."

He laughed. He didn't seem to be very much afraid of Mrs. Batt.

It had grown deliciously dusky, and myriads of stars were

coming out. Little by little the lake lost its shape in the darkness, until only an irregular, star-set area of quiet water indicated that there was any lake there at all.

I remember that Brown and I, reclining at the foot of the tree, were looking at the still and starry surface of the lake, over which numbers of bats were darting after insects; and I recollect that I was just about to speak, when, of a sudden, the silent and luminous surface of the water was shattered as with a subterranean explosion; a geyser of scintillating spray shot upward flashing, foaming, towering a hundred feet into the air. And through it I seemed to catch a glimpse of a vast, quivering, twisting mass of silver falling back with a crash into the lake, while the huge fountain rained spray on every side and the little lake rocked and heaved from shore to shore, sending great sheets of surf up over the rocks so high that the very tree-tops dripped.

Petrified, dumb, our senses almost paralyzed by the shock, our ears still deafened by the watery crash of that gigantic something that had fallen into the lake, and our eyes starting from their sockets, we stared at the darkness.

Slap—slash—slush went the waves, hitting the shore with a clashing sound almost metallic. Vision and hearing told us that the water in the lake was rocking like the contents of a bath-tub.

"G-g-good Lord!" whispered Brown. "Is there a v-volcano under that lake?"

"Did you see that huge, glittering shape that seemed to fall into the water?" I gasped.

"Yes. What was it? A meteor?"

"No. It was something that first came out of the lake and fell back—the way a trout leaps. Heavens! It couldn't have been alive, could it?"

"W-wh-what do you mean?" stammered Brown.

"It couldn't have been a f-f-fish, could it?" I asked with chattering teeth.

"No! No! It was as big as a Pullman car! It must have been a falling star. Did you ever hear of a fish as big as a sleeping car?"

I was too thoroughly unnerved to reply. The roaring of the surf had subsided somewhat, enough for another sound to reach our ears—a raucous, gallinacious, squawking sound.

I sprang up and looked at the row of tents. White-robed figures loomed in front of them. The heavy artillery was evidently frightened.

We went over to them, and when we got nearer they chastely scuttled into their tents and thrust out a row of heads—heads hideous with curl-papers.

50

"What was that awful noise? An earthquake?" shrilled the Reverend Dr. Jones. "I think I'll go home."

"Was it an avalanche?" demanded Mrs. Batt, in a deep and shaky voice. "Are we in any immediate danger, young man?"

I said that it was probably a flying-star which had happened to strike the lake and explode.

"What an awful region!" wailed Miss Dingleheimer. "I've had my money's worth. I wish to go back to New York at once. I'll begin to dress immediately—"

"It might be a million years before another meteor falls in this latitude," I said, soothingly.

"Or it might be ten minutes," sobbed Miss Dingleheimer. "What do you know about it, anyway! I want to go home. I'm putting on my stockings now. I'm getting dressed as fast as I can—"

Her voice was blotted out in a mighty crash from the lake. Appalled, I whirled on my heel, just in time to see another huge jet of water rise high in the starlight, another, another, until the entire lake was but a cluster of gigantic geysers exploding a hundred feet in the air, while through them, falling back into the smother of furious foam, great silvery bulks dropped crashing, one after another.

I don't know how long the incredible vision lasted; the woods roared with the infernal pandemonium, echoed and re-echoed from mountain to mountain; the tree-tops fairly stormed spray, driving it in sheets through the leaves; and the shores of the lake spouted surf long after the last vast, silvery shape had fallen back again into the water.

As my senses gradually recovered, I found myself supporting Mrs. Batt on one arm and the Reverend Dr. Jones upon my bosom. Both had fainted. I released them with a shudder and turned to look for Brown.

He was not noticing me, and as I approached him I heard him say something resembling the word "kitten."

In spite of my demoralization, another fear seized me, and I drew nearer and peered closely at what he was holding so nobly in his arms. It was, as I supposed, Angelica White.

I don't know whether my arrival occultly revived her, for as I stumbled over a tent-peg she opened her blue eyes, and then disengaged herself from Brown's arms.

"Oh, I am so frightened," she murmured. She looked at me sideways when she said it.

"Come," said I coldly to Brown, "let Miss White retire and lie down. This meteoric shower is over and so is the danger."

He evinced a desire to further soothe and minister to Miss

White, but she said, with considerable composure, that she was feeling better; and Brown came unwillingly with me to inspect the heavy artillery lines.

That formidable battery was wrecked, the pieces dismounted and lying tumbled about in their emplacements.

But a vigorous course of cold water in dippers revived them, and we herded them into one tent and quieted them with some soothing prevarication, the details of which I have forgotten; but it was something about a flock of meteors which hit the earth every twelve billion years, and that it was now all over for another such interim, and everybody could sleep soundly with the consciousness of having assisted at a spectacle never before beheld except by a primordial protoplasmic cell.

Which flattered them, I think, for, seated once more at the base of our tree, presently we heard weird noises from the reconcentrados, like the moaning of the harbour bar.

They slept, the heavy guns, like unawakened engines of destruction all a-row in battery. But Brown and I, fearfully excited, still dazed and bewildered, sat with our fascinated eyes fixed on the lake, asking each other what in the name of miracles it was that we had witnessed and heard.

On one thing we were agreed. A scientific discovery of the most enormous importance awaited our investigation.

This was no time for temporising, for deception, for any species of polite shilly-shallying. We must, on the morrow, tear off our masks and appear before these misguided and feminine victims of our duplicity in our own characters as scientists. We must boldly avow our identities and flatly refuse to stir from this spot until the mystery of this astounding lake had been thoroughly investigated.

And so, discussing our policy, our plans for the morrow, and mutually reassuring each other concerning our common ability to successfully defy the heavy artillery, we finally fell asleep.

III

Dawn awoke me, and I sat up in my blanket and aroused Brown.

No birds were singing. It seemed unusual, and I spoke of it to

Brown. Never have I witnessed such a still, strange daybreak. Mountains, woods, and water were curiously silent. There was not a sound to be heard, nothing stirred except the thin veil of vapour over the water, shreds of which were now parting from the shore and steaming slowly upward.

There was, it seemed to me, something slightly uncanny about this lake, even in repose. The water seemed as translucent as a dark crystal, and as motionless as the surface of a mirror. Nothing stirred its placid surface, not a ripple, not an insect, not a leaf floating.

Brown had lugged the pneumatic raft down to the shore where he was now pumping it full: I followed with the paddles, pole, and hydroscope. When the raft had been pumped up and was afloat, we carried the reel of gossamer piano-wire aboard, followed it, pushed off, and paddled quietly through the level cobwebs of mist toward the centre of the lake. From the shore I heard a gruesome noise. It originated under one of the row of tents of the heavy artillery. Medusa, snoring, was an awesome sound in that wilderness and solitude of dawn.

I was unscrewing the centre-plug from the raft and screwing into the empty socket the lens of the hydroscope and attaching the battery, while Brown started his sounding; and I was still busy when an exclamation from my companion started me:

"We're breaking some records! Do you know it, Smith?"

"Where is the lead?"

"Three hundred fathoms and still running!"

"Nonsense!"

"Look at it yourself! It goes on unreeling: I've put the drag on. Hurry and adjust the hydroscope!"

I sighted the powerful instrument for two thousand feet, altering it from minute to minute as Brown excitedly announced the amazing depth of the lake. When he called out four thousand feet, I stared at him.

"There's something wrong—" I began.

"There's nothing wrong!" he interrupted. "Four thousand five hundred! Five thousand! Five thousand five hundred—"

"Are you squatting there and trying to tell me that this lake is over a mile deep!"

"Look for yourself!" he said in an unsteady voice. "Here is the tape! You can read, can't you? Six thousand feet—and running evenly. Six thousand five hundred!... Seven thousand! Seven thousand five—"

"It can't be!" I protested.

But it was true. Astounded, I continued to adjust the hydroscope to a range incredible, turning the screw to focus at a mile and a half, at two miles, at two and a quarter, a half, three-quarters, three miles, three miles and a quarter—click!

"Good Heavens!" he whispered. "This lake is three miles and a quarter deep!"

Mechanically I set the lachet, screwed the hood firm, drew out the black eye-mask, locked it, then, kneeling on the raft I rested my face in the mask, felt for the lever, and switched on the electric light.

Quicker than thought the solid lance of dazzling light plunged down through profundity, and the vast abyss of water was revealed along its pathway.

Nothing moved in those tremendous depths except, nearly two miles below, a few spots of tinsel glittered and drifted like flakes of mica.

At first I scarcely noticed them, supposing them to be vast beds of silvery bottom sand glittering under the electric pencil of the hydroscope. But presently it occurred to me that these brilliant specks in motion were not on the bottom—were a little less than two miles deep, and therefore suspended.

To be seen at all, at two miles' depth, whatever they were they must have considerable bulk.

"Do you see anything?" demanded Brown.

"Some silvery specks at a depth of two miles."

"What do they look like?"

"Specks."

"Are they in motion?"

"They seem to be."

"Do they come any nearer?"

After a while I answered:

"One of the specks seems to be growing larger.... I believe it is in motion and is floating slowly upward.... It's certainly getting bigger.... It's getting longer."

"Is it a fish?"

"It can't be."

"Why not?"

"It's impossible. Fish don't attain the size of whales in mountain ponds."

There was a silence. After an interval I said:

"Brown, I don't know what to make of that thing."

"Is it coming any nearer?"

"Yes."

"What does it look like now?"

"It looks like a fish. But it can't be. It looks like a tiny, silver minnow. But it can't be. Why, if it resembles a minnow in size at this distance—what can be its actual dimensions?"

"Let me look," he said.

Unwillingly I raised my head from the mask and yielded him my place.

A long silence followed. The western mountain-tops reddened under the rising sun; the sky grew faintly bluer. Yet, there was not a bird-note in that still place, not a flash of wings, nothing stirring.

Here and there along the lake shore I noticed unusual-looking trees—very odd-looking trees indeed, for their trunks seemed bleached and dead, and as though no bark covered them, yet every stark limb was covered with foliage—a thick foliage so dark in colour that it seemed black to me.

I glanced at my motionless companion where he knelt with his face in the mask, then I unslung my field-glasses and focussed them on the nearest of the curious trees.

At first I could not quite make out what I was looking at; then, to my astonishment, I saw that these stark, gray trees were indeed lifeless, and that what I had mistaken for dark foliage were velvety clusters of bats hanging there asleep—thousands of them thickly infesting and clotting the dead branches with a sombre and horrid effect of foliage.

I don't mind bats in ordinary numbers. But in such soft, motionless masses they slightly sickened me. There must have been literally tons of them hanging to the dead trees.

"This is pleasant," I said. "Look at those bats, Brown."

When Brown spoke without lifting his head, his voice was so shaken, so altered, that the mere sound of it scared me:

"Smith," he said, "there is a fish in here, shaped exactly like a brook minnow. And I should judge, by the depth it is swimming in, that it is about as long as an ordinary Pullman car."

His voice shook, but his words were calm to the point of commonplace. Which made the effect of his statement all the more terrific.

"A—a minnow—as big as a Pullman car?" I repeated, dazed.

"Larger, I think.... It looks to me through the hydroscope, at this distance, exactly like a tiny, silvery minnow. It's half a mile down.... Swimming about.... I can see its eyes; they must be about ten feet in diameter. I can see its fins moving. And there are about a dozen others, much deeper, swimming around.... This is easily the most overwhelming contribution made to science since the discovery of the purple-spotted dingle-bock, Bukkus dinglii.... We've got to catch one of those gigantic fish!"

"How?" I gasped. "How are we going to catch a minnow as large as a sleeping car?"

"I don't know, but we've got to do it. We've got to manage it, somehow."

"It would require a steel cable to hold such a fish and a donkey engine to reel him in! And what about a hook? And if we had hook, line, steam-winch, and everything else, what about bait?"

He knelt for some time longer, watching the fish, before he resigned the hydroscope to me. Then I watched it; but it came no nearer, seeming contented to swim about at the depth of a little more than half a mile. Deep under this fish I could see others glittering as they sailed or darted to and fro.

Presently I raised my head and sat thinking. The sun now gilded the water; a little breeze ruffled it here and there where dainty cat's-paws played over the surface.

"What on earth do you suppose those gigantic fish feed on?" asked Brown under his breath.

I thought a moment longer, then it came to me in a flash of understanding, and I pointed at the dead trees.

"Bats!" I muttered. "They feed on bats as other fish feed on the little, gauzy-winged flies which dance over ponds! You saw those bats flying over the pond last night, didn't you? That explains the whole thing! Don't you understand? Why, what we saw were these gigantic fish leaping like trout after the bats. It was their feeding time!"

I do not imagine that two more excited scientists ever existed than Brown and I. The joy of discovery transfigured us. Here we had discovered a lake in the Thunder Mountains which was the deepest lake in the world; and it was inhabited by a few gigantic fish of the minnow species, the existence of which, hitherto, had never even been dreamed of by science.

"Kitten," I said, my voice broken by emotion, "which will you have named after you, the lake or the fish? Shall it be Lake Kitten Brown, or shall it be Minnius kittenii? Speak!"

"What about that old party whose name you said had already been given to the lake?" he asked piteously.

"Who? Mrs. Batt? Do you think I'd name such an important lake after her? Anyway, she has declined the honour."

"Very well," he said, "I'll accept it. And the fish shall be known as Minnius Smithii!"

Too deeply moved to speak, we bent over and shook hands with each other. In that solemn and holy moment, surcharged with ecstatic emotion, a deep, distant reverberation came across the water to our ears. It was the heavy artillery, snoring.

Never can I forget that scene; sunshine glittering on the pond, the silent forests and towering peaks, the blue sky overhead, the dead trees where thousands of bats hung in nauseating clusters, thicker than the leaves in Valembrosa—and Kitten Brown and I, cross-legged upon our pneumatic raft, hands clasped in pledge of deathless devotion to science and a fraternity unending.

"And how about that girl?" he asked.

"What girl?"

"Angelica White?"

"Well," said I, "what about her?"

"Does she go with the lake or with the fish?"

"What do you mean?" I asked coldly, withdrawing my hand from his clasp.

"I mean, which of us gets the first chance to win her?" he said, blushing. "There's no use denying that we both have been bowled over by her; is there?"

I pondered for several moments.

"She is an extremely intelligent girl," I said, stalling.

"Yes, and then some."

After a few minutes' further thought, I said:

"Possibly I am in error, but at moments it has seemed to me that my marked attentions to Miss White are not wholly displeasing to her. I may be mistaken—"

"I think you are, Smith."

"Why?"

"Because—well, because I seem to think so."

I said coldly:

"Because she happened to faint away in your arms last night is no symptom that she prefers you. Is it?"

"No."

"Then why do you seem to think that tactful, delicate, and assiduous attentions on my part may prove not entirely unwelcome to this unusually intelligent—"

"Smith!"

"What?"

"Miss White is not only a trained nurse, but she also is about to receive her diploma as a physician."

"How do you know?"

"She told me."

"When?"

"When you were building the fire last night. Also, she informed me that she had relentlessly dedicated herself to a eugenic marriage."

"When did she tell you that?"

"While you were bringing in a bucket of water from the lake last night. And furthermore, she told me that I was perfectly suited for a eugenic marriage."

"When did she tell you that?" I demanded.

"When she had—fainted—in my arms."

"How the devil did she come to say a thing like that?"

He became conspicuously red about the ears:

"Well, I had just told her that I had fallen in love with her—"

"Damn!" I said. And that's all I said; and seizing a paddle I made furiously for shore. Behind me I heard the whirr of the piano wire as Brown started the electric reel. Later I heard him clamping the hood on the hydroscope; but I was too disgusted for any further words, and I dug away at the water with my paddle.

In various and weird stages of morning déshabillé the heavy artillery came down to the shore for morning ablutions, all a-row like a file of ducks.

They glared at me as I leaped ashore:

"I want my breakfast!" snapped Mrs. Batt. "Do you hear what I say, guide? And I don't wish to be kept waiting for it either! I desire to get out of this place as soon as possible."

"I'm sorry," I said, "but I intend to stay here for some time."

"What!" bawled the heavy artillery in booming unison.

But my temper had been sorely tried, and I was in a mood to tell the truth and make short work of it, too.

"Ladies," I said, "I'll not mince matters. Mr. Brown and I are not guides; we are scientists from Bronx Park, and we don't know a bally thing about this wilderness we're in!"

"Swindler!" shouted Mrs. Batt, in an enraged voice. "I knew very well that the United States Government would never have named that puddle of water after me!"

"Don't worry, madam! I've named it after Mr. Brown. And the new species of gigantic fish which I discovered in this lake I have named after myself. As for leaving this spot until I have concluded my scientific study of these fish, I simply won't. I intend to observe their habits and to capture one of them if it requires the remainder of my natural life to do so. I shall be sorry to detain you here during such a period, but it can't be helped. And now you know what the situation is, and you are at liberty to think it over after you have washed your countenances in Lake Kitten Brown."

Rage possessed the heavy artillery, and a fury indescribable seized them when they discovered that Indians had raided their half ton of feminine perquisites. I went up a tree.

When the tumult had calmed sufficiently for them to distinguish what I said, I made a speech to them. From the higher branches of a neighboring tree Kitten Brown applauded and cried, "Hear! Hear!"

"Ladies," I said, "you know the worst, now. If you keep me up this tree and starve me to death it will be murder. Also, you don't know enough to get out of these forests, but I can guide you back the way you came. I'll do it if you cease your dangerous demonstrations and permit Mr. Brown and myself to remain here and study these giant fish for a week or two."

They now seemed disposed to consider the idea. There was nothing else for them to do. So after an hour or two, Brown and I ventured to descend from our trees, and we went among them to placate them and ingratiate ourselves as best we might.

"Think," I argued, "what a matchless opportunity for you to be among the first discoverers of a totally new and undescribed species of giant fish! Think what a legacy it will be to leave such a record to posterity! Think how proud and happy your descendants will be to know that their ancestors assisted at the discovery of Minnius Smithii!"

"Why can't they be named after me?" demanded Mrs. Batt.

"Because," I explained patiently, "they have already been named after me!"

"Couldn't something be named after me?" inquired that fearsome lady.

"The bats," suggested Brown politely, "we could name a bat after you with pleasure—"

I thought for a moment she meant to swing on him. He thought so, too, and ducked.

"A bat!" she shouted. "Name a bat after me!"

"Many a celebrated scientist has been honoured by having his name conferred upon humbler fauna," I explained.

But she remained dangerous, so I went and built the fire, and squatted there, frying bacon, while on the other side of the fire, sitting side by side, Kitten Brown and Angelica White gazed upon each other with enraptured eyes. It was slightly sickening—but let that pass. I was beginning to understand that science is a jealous mistress and that any contemplated infidelity of mine stood every chance of being squelched. No; evidently I had not been fashioned for the joys of legal domesticity. Science, the wanton jade, had not yet finished her dance with me. Apparently my maxixe with her was to be external. Fides servanda est.

That afternoon the heavy artillery held a council of war, and evidently came to a conclusion to make the best of the situation, for toward sundown they accosted me with a request for the raft, explaining that they desired to picnic aboard and afterward row about the lake and indulge in song.

So Brown and I put aboard the craft a substantial cold supper; and the heavy artillery embarked, taking aboard a guitar to be worked by Miss Dingleheimer, and knitting for the others.

It was a lovely evening. Brown and I had been discussing a plan to dynamite the lake and stun the fish, that method appealing to us as the only possible way to secure a specimen of the stupendous minnows which inhabited the depths. In fact, it was our only hope of possessing one of these creatures—fishing with a donkey engine, steel cable, and a hook baited with a bat being too uncertain and far more laborious and expensive.

I was still smoking my pipe, seated at the foot of the big pine-tree, watching the water turn from gold to pink: Brown sat higher up the slope, his arm around Angelica White. I carefully kept my back toward them.

On the lake the heavy artillery were revelling loudly, banqueting, singing, strumming the guitar, and trailing their hands overboard across the sunset-tinted water.

I was thinking of nothing in particular as I now remember, except that I noticed the bats beginning to flit over the lake; when Brown called to me from the slope above, asking whether it was perfectly safe for the heavy artillery to remain out so late.

"Why?" I demanded.

"Suppose," he shouted, "that those fish should begin to jump and feed on the bats again?"

I had never thought of that.

I rose and hurried nervously down to the shore, and, making a megaphone of my hands, I shouted:

"Come in! It isn't safe to remain out any longer!"

Scornful laughter from the artillery answered my appeal.

"You'd better come in!" I called. "You can't tell what might happen if any of those fish should jump."

"Mind your business!" retorted Mrs. Batt. "We've had enough of your prevarications—"

Then, suddenly, without the faintest shadow of warning, from the centre of the lake a vast geyser of water towered a hundred feet in the air.

For one dreadful second I saw the raft hurled skyward, balanced on the crest of the stupendous fountain, spilling ladies, supper, guitars, and knitting in every direction.

Then a horrible thing occurred; fish after fish shot up out of the storm of water and foam, seizing, as they fell, ladies, luncheon, and knitting in mid-air, falling back with a crashing shock which seemed to rock the very mountains.

"Help!" I screamed. And fainted dead away.

Is it necessary to proceed? Literature nods; Science shakes her head. No, nothing but literature lies beyond the ripples which splashed musically upon the shore, terminating forever the last vibration from that immeasurable catastrophe.

Why should I go on? The newspapers of the nation have recorded the last scenes of the tragedy.

We know that tons of dynamite are being forwarded to that solitary lake. We know that it is the determination of the Government to rid the world of those gigantic minnows.

And yet, somehow, it seems to me as I sit writing here in my office, amid the verdure of Bronx Park, that the destruction of these enormous fish is a mistake.

What more splendid sarcophagus could the ladies of the lake desire than these huge, silvery, itinerant and living tombs?

What reward more sumptuous could anybody wish for than to rest at last within the interior dimness of an absolutely new species of anything?

For me, such a final repose as this would represent the highest pinnacle of sublimity, the uttermost zenith of mortal dignity.

So what more is there for me to say?

As for Angelica—but no matter. I hope she may be comparatively happy with Kitten Brown. Yet, as I have said before, handsome men never last. But she should have thought of that in time.

I absolve myself of all responsibility. She had her chance.

ONE OVER

I

Professor Farrago had remarked to me that morning:

"The city of New York always reminds me of a slovenly, fat woman with her dress unbuttoned behind."

I nodded.

"New York's architecture," said I, "—or what popularly passes for it—is all in front. The minute you get to the rear a pitiable condition is exposed."

He said: "Professor Jane Bottomly is all façade; the remainder of her is merely an occipital backyard full of theoretical tin cans and broken bottles. I think we all had better resign."

It was a fearsome description. I trembled as I lighted an inexpensive cigar.

The sentimental feminist movement in America was clearly at the bottom of the Bottomly affair.

Long ago, in a reactionary burst of hysteria, the North enfranchised the Ethiopian. In a similar sentimental explosion of dementia, some sixty years later, the United States wept violently over the immemorial wrongs perpetrated upon the restless sex, opened the front and back doors of opportunity, and sobbed out, "Go to it, ladies!"

They are still going.

Professor Jane Bottomly was wished on us out of a pleasant April sky. She fell like a meteoric mass of molten metal upon the Bronx Park Zoölogical Society splashing her excoriating personality over everybody until everybody writhed.

I had not yet seen the lady. I did not care to. Sooner or later I'd be obliged to meet her but I was not impatient.

Now the Field Expeditionary Force of the Bronx Park Zoölogical Society is, perhaps, the most important arm of the service. Professor Bottomly had just been appointed official head of all field work. Why? Nobody knew. It is true that she had written several combination nature and love romances. In these popular volumes trees, flowers, butterflies, birds, animals, dialect, sobs, and sun-bonnets were stirred up together into a saccharine mess eagerly gulped down by a provincial reading public, which immediately protruded its tongue for more.

The news of her impending arrival among us was an awful blow to everybody at the Bronx. Professor Farrago fainted in the arms of his pretty stenographer; Professor Cornelius Lezard of the Batrachian Department ran around his desk all day long in narrowing circles and was discovered on his stomach still feebly squirming like an expiring top; Dr. Hans Fooss, our beloved Professor of Pachydermatology sat for hours weeping into his noodle soup. As for me, I was both furious and frightened, for, within the hearing of several people, Professor Bottomly had remarked in a very clear voice to her new assistant, Dr. Daisy Delmour, that she intended to get rid of me for the good of the Bronx because of my reputation for indiscreet gallantry among the feminine employees of the Bronx Society.

Professor Lezard overhead that outrageous remark and he hastened to repeat it to me.

I was lunching at the time in my private office in the Administration Building with Dr. Hans Fooss—he and I being too busy dissecting an unusually fine specimen of Dingue to go to the Rolling Stone Inn for luncheon—when Professor Lezard rushed in with the scandalous libel still sizzling in his ears.

"Everybody heard her say it!" he went on, wringing his hands. "It was a most unfortunate thing for anybody to say about you before all those young ladies. Every stenographer and typewriter there turned pale and then red."

"What!" I exclaimed, conscious that my own ears were growing large and hot. "Did that outrageous woman have the bad taste to say such a thing before all those sensitive girls!"

"She did. She glared at them when she said it. Several blondes and one brunette began to cry."

"I hope," said I, a trifle tremulously, "that no typewriter so far forgot herself as to admit noticing playfulness on my part."

"They all were tearfully unanimous in declaring you to be a perfect gentleman!"

"I am," I said. "I am also a married man—irrevocably wedded to science. I desire no other spouse. I am ineligible; and everybody knows it. If at times a purely scientific curiosity leads me into a detached and impersonally psychological investigation of certain—ah—feminine idiosyncrasies—"

"Certainly," said Lezard. "To investigate the feminine is more than a science; it is a duty!"

"Of a surety!" nodded Dr. Fooss.

I looked proudly upon my two loyal friends and bit into my

cheese sandwich. Only men know men. A jury of my peers had exonerated me. What did I care for Professor Bottomly!

"All the same," added Lezard, "you'd better be careful or Professor Bottomly will put one over on you yet."

"I am always careful," I said with dignity.

"All men should be. It is the only protection of a defenseless coast line," nodded Lezard.

"Und neffer, neffer commid nodding to paper," added Dr. Fooss. "Don'd neffer write it, 'I lofe you like I was going to blow up alretty!' Ach, nein! Don'd you write down somedings. Effery man he iss entitled to protection; und so iss it he iss protected."

Stein in hand he beamed upon us benevolently over his knifeful of sauerfisch, then he fed himself and rammed it down with a hearty draught of Pilsner. We gazed with reverence upon Kultur as embodied in this great Teuton.

"That woman," remarked Lezard to me, "certainly means to get rid of you. It seems to me that there are only two possible ways for you to hold down your job at the Bronx. You know it, don't you?"

I nodded. "Yes," I said; "either I must pay marked masculine attention to Professor Bottomly or I must manage to put one over on her."

"Of course," said Lezard, "the first method is the easier for you—"

"Not for a minute!" I said, hastily; "I simply couldn't become frolicsome with her. You say she's got a voice like a drill-sergeant and she goose-steps when she walks; and I don't mind admitting she has me badly scared already. No; she must be scientifically ruined. It is the only method which makes her elimination certain."

"But if her popular nature books didn't ruin her scientifically, how can we hope to lead her astray?" inquired Lezard.

"There is," I said, thoughtfully, "only one thing that can really ruin a scientist. Ridicule! I have braved it many a time, taking my scientific life in my hands in pursuit of unknown specimens which might have proved only imaginary. Public ridicule would have ended my scientific career in such an event. I know of no better way to end Professor Bottomly's scientific career and capability for mischief than to start her out after something which doesn't exist, inform the newspapers, and let her suffer the agonising consequences."

Dr. Fooss began to shout:

"The idea iss schön! colossal! prachtvol! ausgezeichnet! wunderbar! wunderschön! gemütlich—" A large, tough noodle checked him. While he labored with Teutonic imperturbability to master it Lezard and I exchanged suggestions regarding the proposed annihilation of this fearsome woman who had come ravening among us amid the peaceful and soporific environment of Bronx Park.

It was a dreadful thing for us to have our balmy Lotus-eaters' paradise so startlingly invaded by a large, loquacious, loud-voiced lady who had already stirred us all out of our agreeable, traditional and leisurely inertia. Inertia begets cogitation, and cogitation begets ideas, and ideas beget reflexion, and profound reflexion is the fundamental cornerstone of that immortal temple in which the goddess Science sits asleep between her dozing sisters, Custom and Religion.

This thought seemed to me so unusually beautiful that I wrote it with a pencil upon my cuff.

While I was writing it, quietly happy in the deep pleasure that my intellectual allegory afforded me, Dr. Fooss swabbed the last morsel of nourishment from his plate with a wad of rye bread, then bolting the bread and wiping his beard with his fingers and his fingers on his waistcoat, he made several guttural observations too profoundly German to be immediately intelligible, and lighted his porcelain pipe.

"Ach wass!" he remarked in ruminative fashion. "Dot Frauenzimmer she iss to raise hell alretty determined. Von Pachydermatology she knows nodding. Maybe she leaves me alone, maybe it is to be 'raus mit me. I' weis' ni'! It iss aber besser one over on dat lady to put, yess?"

"It certainly is advisable," replied Lezard.

"Let us try to think of something sufficiently disastrous to terminate her scientific career," said I. And I bowed my rather striking head and rested the point of my forefinger upon my forehead. Thought crystallises more quickly for me when I assume this attitude.

Out of the corner of my eye I saw Lezard fold his arms and sit frowning at infinity.

Dr. Fooss lay back in a big, deeply padded armchair and closed his prominent eyes. His pipe went out presently, and now and then he made long-drawn nasal remarks, in German, too complicated for either Lezard or for me to entirely comprehend.

"We must try to get her as far away from here as possible," mused Lezard. "Is Oyster Bay too far and too cruel?"

I pondered darkly upon the suggestion. But it seemed unpleasantly like murder.

"Lezard," said I, "come, let us reason together. Now what is woman's besetting emotion?"

"Curiosity?"

"Very well; assuming that to be true, what—ah—quality particularly characterizes woman when so beset."

"Ruthless determination."

"Then," said I, "we ought to begin my exciting the curiosity of Professor Bottomly; and her ruthless determination to satisfy that curiosity should logically follow."

"How," he asked, "are we to arouse her curiosity?"

"By pretending that we have knowledge of something hitherto undiscovered, the discovery of which would redound to our scientific glory."

"I see. She'd want the glory for herself. She'd swipe it."

"She would," said I.

"Tee—hee!" he giggled; "Wouldn't it be funny to plant something phony on her—"

I waved my arms rather gracefully in my excitement:

"That is the germ of an idea!" I said. "If we could plant something—something—far away from here—very far away—if we could bury something—like the Cardiff Giant—"

"Hundreds and hundreds of miles away!"

"Thousands!" I insisted, enthusiastically.

"Tee-hee! In Tasmania, for example! Maybe a Tasmanian Devil might acquire her!"

"There exists a gnat," said I, "in Borneo—Gnatus soporificus— and when this tiny gnat stings people they never entirely wake up. It's really rather a pleasurable catastrophe, I understand. Life becomes one endless cat-nap—one delightful siesta, with intervals for light nourishment.... She—ah—could sit very comfortably in some pleasant retreat and rock in a rocking-chair and doze quite happily through the years to come.... And from your description of her I should say that the Soldiers' Home might receive her."

"It won't do," he said, gloomily.

"Why? Is it too much like crime?"

"Oh not at all. Only if she went to Borneo she'd be sure to take a mosquito-bar with her."

In the depressed silence which ensued Dr. Fooss suddenly made several Futurist observations through his nose with monotonous but authoritative regularity. I tried to catch his meaning and his eye. The one remained cryptic, the other shut.

Lezard sat thinking very hard. And as I fidgetted in my chair, fiddling nervously with various objects lying on my desk I chanced to pick up a letter from the pile of still unopened mail at my elbow.

Still pondering on Professor Bottomly's proposed destruction, I turned the letter over idly and my preoccupied gaze rested on the postmark. After a moment I leaned forward and examined it more attentively. The letter directed to me was postmarked Fort Carcajou, Cook's Peninsula, Baffin Land; and now I recalled the handwriting, having already seen it three or four times within the last month or so.

"Lezard," I said, "that lunatic trapper from Baffin Land has written to me again. What do you suppose is the matter with him? Is he just plain crazy or does he think he can be funny with me?"

Lezard gazed at me absently. Then, all at once a gleam of savage interest lighted his somewhat solemn features.

"Read the letter to me," he said, with an evil smile which instantly animated my own latent imagination. And immediately it occurred to me that perhaps, in the humble letter from the wilds of Baffin Land, which I was now opening with eager and unsteady fingers, might lie concealed the professional undoing of Professor Jane Bottomly, and the only hope of my own ultimate and scientific salvation.

The room became hideously still as I unfolded the pencil-scrawled sheets of cheap, ruled letter paper.

Dr. Fooss opened his eyes, looked at me, made porcine sounds indicative of personal well-being, relighted his pipe, and disposed himself to listen. But just as I was about to begin, Lezard suddenly laid his forefinger across his lips conjuring us to densest silence.

For a moment or two I heard nothing except the buzzing of flies. Then I stole a startled glance at my door. It was opening slowly, almost imperceptibly.

But it did not open very far—just a crack remained. Then, listening with all our might, we heard the cautiously suppressed breathing of somebody in the hallway just outside of my door.

Lezard turned and cast at me a glance of horrified intelligence. In dumb pantomime he outlined in the air, with one hand, the large and feminine amplification of his own person, conveying to us the certainty of his suspicions concerning the unseen eavesdropper.

We nodded. We understood perfectly that she was out there prepared to listen to every word we uttered.

A flicker of ferocious joy disturbed Lezard's otherwise innocuous features; he winked horribly at Dr. Fooss and at me, and uttered a faint click with his teeth and tongue like the snap of a closing trap.

"Gentlemen," he said, in the guarded yet excited voice of a man who is confident of not being overheard, "the matter under discussion admits of only one interpretation: a discovery—perhaps the most vitally important discovery of all the centuries—is imminent.

"Secrecy is imperative; the scientific glory is to be shared by us alone, and there is enough of glory to go around.

"Mr. Chairman, I move that epoch-making letter be read aloud!"

"I second dot motion!" said Dr. Fooss, winking so violently at me that his glasses wabbled.

"Gentlemen," said I, "it has been moved and seconded that this epoch-making letter be read aloud. All those in favor will kindly say 'aye.'"

"Aye! Aye!" they exclaimed, fairly wriggling in their furtive joy.

"The contrary-minded will kindly emit the usual negation," I went on.... "It seems to be carried.... It is carried. The chairman will proceed to the reading of the epoch-making letter."

I quietly lighted a five-cent cigar, unfolded the letter and read aloud:

"Joneses Shack,

Golden Glacier, Cook's Peninsula, Baffin Land,
March 15, 1915.
"Professor, Dear Sir:
"I already wrote you three times no answer having been rec'd perhaps you think I'm kiddin' you're a dam' liar I ain't.
"Hoping to tempt you to come I will hereby tell you more'n I told you in my other letters, the terminal moraine of this here Golden Glacier finishes into a marsh, nothing to see for miles excep' frozen tussock and mud and all flat as hell for fifty miles which is where I am trappin' it for mink and otter and now ready to go back to Fort Carcajou. i told you what I seen stickin' in under this here marsh, where anything sticks out the wolves have eat it, but most of them there ellerphants is in under the ice and mud too far for the wolves to git 'em.
"i ain't kiddin' you, there is a whole herd of furry ellerphants in the marsh like as they were stuck there and all lay down and was drownded like. Some has tusks and some hasn't. Two ellerphants stuck out of the ice, I eat onto one, the meat was good and sweet and joosy, the damn wolves eat it up that night, I had cut stakes and rost for three months though and am eating off it yet.
"Thinking as how ellerphants and all like that is your graft, I being a keeper in the Mouse House once in the Bronx and seein' you nosin' around like you was full of

scientific thinks, it comes to me to write you and put you next.

"If you say so I'll wait here and help you with them ellerphants. Livin' wages is all I ask also eleven thousand dollars for tippin' you wise. I won't tell nobody till I hear from you. I'm hones' you can trus' me. Write me to Fort Carcajou if you mean bizness. So no more respectfully,

James Skaw."

When I finished reading I cautiously glanced at the door, and, finding it still on the crack, turned and smiled subtly upon Lezard and Fooss.

In their slowly spreading grins I saw they agreed with me that somebody, signing himself James Skaw, was still trying to hoax the Great Zoölogical Society of Bronx Park.

"Gentlemen," I said aloud, injecting innocent enthusiasm into my voice, "this secret expedition to Baffin Land which we three are about to organise is destined to be without doubt the most scientifically prolific field expedition ever organised by man.

"Imagine an entire herd of mammoths preserved in mud and ice through all these thousands of years!

"Gentlemen, no discovery ever made has even remotely approached in importance the discovery made by this simple, illiterate trapper, James Skaw."

"I thought," protested Lezard, "that we are to be announced as the discoverers."

"We are," said I, "the discoverers of James Skaw, which makes us technically the finders of the ice-preserved herd of mammoths— technically, you understand. A few thousand dollars," I added, carelessly, "ought to satiate James Skaw."

"We could name dot glacier after him," suggested Dr. Fooss.

"Certainly—the Skaw Glacier. That ought to be enough glory for him. It ought to satisfy him and prevent any indiscreet remarks," nodded Lezard.

"Gentlemen," said I, "there is only one detail that really troubles me. Ought we to notify our honoured and respected Chief of Division concerning this discovery?"

"Do you mean, should we tell that accomplished and fascinating lady, Professor Bottomly, about this herd of mammoths?" I asked in a loud, clear voice. And immediately answered my own question: "No," I said, "no, dear friends. Professor Bottomly already has too much responsibility weighing upon her distinguished mind. No, dear brothers in science, we should steal away unobserved as though setting out upon an ordinary field expedition. And when we return with fresh and immortal laurels such as no man before has ever worn, no doubt that our generous-minded Chief of Division will weave for us further wreaths to crown our brows—the priceless garlands of professional approval!" And I made a horrible face at my co-conspirators.

Before I finished Lezard had taken his own face in his hands for the purpose of stifling raucous and untimely mirth. As for Dr. Fooss, his small, porcine eyes snapped and twinkled madly behind his spectacles, but he seemed rather inclined to approve my flowers of rhetoric.

"Ja," said he, "so iss it besser oursellufs dot gefrozenss herd von elephanten to discover, und, by and by, die elephanten bei der Pronx Bark home yet again once more to bring. We shall therefore much praise thereby bekommen. Ach wass!"

"Gentlemen," said I, distinctly, "it is decided, then, that we shall say nothing concerning the true object of this expedition to Professor Bottomly."

Lezard and Fooss nodded assent. Then, in the silence, we all strained our ears to listen. And presently we detected the scarcely heard sound of cautiously retreating footsteps down the corridor.

When it was safe to do so I arose and closed my door.

"I think," said I, with a sort of infernal cheerfulness in my tones, "that we are about to do something jocose to Jane Bottomly."

"A few," said Professor Lezard. He rose and silently executed a complicated ballet-step.

"I shall laff," said Dr. Fooss, earnestly, "und I shall laff, und I shall laff—ach Gott how I shall laff my pally head off!"

I folded my arms and turned romanesquely toward the direction in which Professor Bottomly had retreated.

"Viper!" I said. "The Bronx shall nourish you in its bosom no more! Fade away, Ophidian!"

The sentiment was applauded by all. There chanced to be in my desk a bottle marked: "That's all!" On the label somebody had written: "Do it now!" We did.

III

It was given out at the Bronx that our field expedition to Baffin Land was to be undertaken solely for the purpose of bringing back living specimens of the five-spotted Arctic woodcock—Philohela quinquemaculata—in order to add to our onomatology and our glossary of onomatopoeia an ontogenesis of this important but hitherto unstudied sub-species.

I trust I make myself clear. Scientific statements should be as clear as the Spuyten Duyvil. Sola in stagno salus!

But two things immediately occurred which worried us; Professor Bottomly sent us official notification that she approved our expedition to Baffin Land, designated the steamer we were to take, and enclosed tickets. That scared us. Then to add to our perplexity Professor Bottomly disappeared, leaving Dr. Daisy Delmour in charge of her department during what she announced might be "a somewhat prolonged absence on business."

And during the four feverish weeks of our pretended preparations for Baffin Land not one word did we hear from Jane Bottomly, which caused us painful inquietude as the hour approached for our departure.

Was this formidable woman actually intending to let us depart alone for the Golden Glacier? Was she too lazy to rob us of the secretly contemplated glory which we had pretended awaited us?

We had been so absolutely convinced that she would forbid our expedition, pack us off elsewhere, and take charge herself of an exploring party to Baffin Land, that, as the time for our leaving drew near we became first uneasy, and then really alarmed.

It would be a dreadful jest on us if she made us swallow our own concoction; if she revealed to our colleagues our pretended knowledge of the Golden Glacier and James Skaw and the supposedly ice-imbedded herd of mammoths, and then publicly forced us to investigate this hoax.

More horrible still would it be if she informed the newspapers and gave them a hint to make merry over the three wise men of the Bronx who went to Baffin Land in a boat.

"What do you suppose that devious and secretive female is up to?" inquired Lezard who, within the last few days, had grown thin with worry. "Is it possible that she is sufficiently degraded to suspect us of trying to put one over on her? Is that what she is now doing to us?"

"Terminus est—it is the limit!" said I.

He turned a morbid eye upon me. "She is making a monkey of us. That's what!"

"Suspendenda omnia naso," I nodded; "tarde sed tute. When I think aloud in Latin it means that I am deeply troubled. Suum quemque scelus agitat. Do you get me, Professor? I'm sorry I attempted to be sportive with this terrible woman. The curse of my scientific career has been periodical excesses of frivolity. See where this frolicsome impulse has landed me!—super abyssum ambulans. Trahit sua quemque voluptas; transeat in exemplum! She means to let us go to our destruction on this mammoth frappé affair."

But Dr. Fooss was optimistic:

"I tink she iss alretty herselluf by dot Baffin Land ge-gone," he said. "I tink she has der bait ge-swallowed. Ve vait; ve see; und so iss it ve know."

"But why hasn't she stopped our preparations?" I demanded. "If she wants all the glory herself why does she permit us to incur this expense in getting ready?"

"No mans can to know der vorkings of der mental brocess by a Frauenzimmer," said Dr. Fooss, wagging his head.

The suspense became nerve-racking; we were obliged to pack our camping kits; and it began to look as though we would have either to sail the next morning or to resign from the Bronx Park Zoölogical Society, because all the evening papers had the story in big type—the details and objects of the expedition, the discovery of the herd of mammoths in cold storage, the prompt organization of an expedition to secure this unparalleled deposit of prehistoric mammalia—everything was there staring at us in violent print, excepting only the name of the discoverer and the names of those composing the field expedition.

"She means to betray us after we have sailed," said Lezard, greatly depressed. "We might just as well resign now before this hoax explodes and bespatters us. We can take our chances in vaudeville or as lecturing professors with the movies."

I thought so, too, in point of fact we all had gathered in my study to write out our resignations, when there came a knock at the door and Dr. Daisy Delmour walked in.

Oddly enough I had not before met Dr. Delmour personally; only formal written communications had hitherto passed between us. My idea of her had doubtless been inspired by the physical and intellectual aberrations of her chief; I naturally supposed her to be either impossible and corporeally redundant, or intellectually and otherwise as weazened as last year's Li-che nut.

I was criminally mistaken. And why Lezard, who knew her, had never set me right I could not then understand. I comprehended later.

For the feminine assistant of Professor Jane Bottomly, who sauntered into my study and announced herself, had the features of Athene, the smile of Aphrodite, and the figure of Psyche. I believe I do not exaggerate these scientific details, although it has been said of me that any pretty girl distorts my vision and my intellectual balance to the detriment of my calmer reason and my differentiating ability.

"Gentlemen," said Dr. Delmour, while we stood in a respectful semi-circle before her, modestly conscious of our worth, our toes turned out, and each man's features wreathed with that politely unnatural smirk which masculine features assume when confronted by feminine beauty. "Gentlemen, on the eve of your proposed departure for Baffin Land in quest of living specimens of the five-spotted Philohela quinquemaculata, I have been instructed by Professor Bottomly to announce to you a great good fortune for her, for you, for the Bronx, for America, for the entire civilized world.

"It has come to Professor Bottomly's knowledge, recently I believe, that an entire herd of mammoths lie encased in the mud and ice of the vast flat marshes which lie south of the terminal moraine of the Golden Glacier in that part of Baffin Land known as Dr. Cook's Peninsula.

"The credit of this epoch-making discovery is Professor Bottomly's entirely. How it happened, she did not inform me. One month ago today she sailed in great haste for Baffin Land. At this very hour she is doubtless standing all alone upon the frozen surface of that wondrous marsh, contemplating with reverence and awe and similar holy emotions the fruits of her own unsurpassed discovery!"

Dr. Delmour's lovely features became delicately suffused and transfigured as she spoke; her exquisite voice thrilled with generous emotion; she clasped her snowy hands and gazed, enraptured, at the picture of Dr. Bottomly which her mind was so charmingly evoking.

"Perhaps," she whispered, "perhaps at this very instant, in the midst of that vast and flat and solemn desolation the only protuberance visible for miles and miles is Professor Bottomly. Perhaps the pallid Arctic sun is setting behind the majestic figure of Professor Bottomly, radiating a blinding glory to the zenith, illuminating the crowning act of her career with its unearthly aura!"

She gazed at us out of dimmed and violet eyes.

"Gentlemen," she said, "I am ordered to take command of this expedition of yours; I am ordered to sail with you tomorrow morning on the Labrador and Baffin Line steamer Dr. Cook.

"The object of your expedition, therefore, is not to be the quest of Philohela quinquemaculata; your duty now is to corroborate the almost miraculous discovery of Professor Bottomly, and to disinter for her the vast herd of frozen mammoths, pack and pickle them, and get them to the Bronx.

"Tomorrow's morning papers will have the entire story: the credit and responsibility for the discovery and the expedition belong to Professor Bottomly, and will be given to her by the press and the populace of our great republic.

"It is her wish that no other names be mentioned. Which is right. To the discoverer belongs the glory. Therefore, the marsh is to be named Bottomly's Marsh, and the Glacier, Bottomly's Glacier.

"Yours and mine is to be the glory of laboring incognito under the direction of the towering scientific intellect of the age, Professor Bottomly.

"And the most precious legacy you can leave your children—if you get married and have any—is that you once wielded the humble pick and shovel for Jane Bottomly on the bottomless marsh which bears her name!"

After a moment's silence we three men ventured to look sideways at each other. We had certainly killed Professor Bottomly, scientifically speaking. The lady was practically dead. The morning papers would consummate the murder. We didn't know whether we wanted to laugh or not.

She was now virtually done for; that seemed certain. So greedily had this egotistical female swallowed the silly bait we offered, so arrogantly had she planned to eliminate everybody excepting herself from the credit of the discovery, that there seemed now nothing left for us to do except to watch her hurdling deliriously toward destruction. Should we burst into hellish laughter?

We looked hard at Dr. Delmour and we decided not to—yet.

Said I: "To assist at the final apotheosis of Professor Bottomly makes us very, very happy. We are happy to remain incognito, mere ciphers blotted out by the fierce white light which is about to beat upon Professor Bottomly, fore and aft. We are happy that our participation in this astonishing affair shall never be known to science.

"But, happiest of all are we, dear Dr. Delmour, in the knowledge that you are to be with us and of us, incognito on this voyage now imminent; that you are to be our revered and beloved leader.

"And I, for one, promise you personally the undivided devotion of a man whose entire and austere career has been dedicated to science—in all its branches."

I stepped forward rather gracefully and raised her little hand to my lips to let her see that even the science of gallantry had not been neglected by me.

Dr. Daisy Delmour blushed.

"Therefore," said I, "considering the fact that our names are not to figure in this expedition; and, furthermore, in consideration of the fact that you are going, we shall be very, very happy to accompany you, Dr. Delmour." I again saluted her hand, and again Dr. Delmour blushed and looked sideways at Professor Lezard.

IV

It was, to be accurate, exactly twenty-three days later that our voyage by sea and land ended one Monday morning upon the gigantic terminal moraine of the Golden Glacier, Cook's Peninsula, Baffin Land.

Four pack-mules carried our luggage, four more bore our persons; an arctic dicky-bird sat on a bowlder and said, "Pilly-willy-willy! Tweet! Tweet!"

As we rode out to the bowlder-strewn edge of the moraine the rising sun greeted us cordially, illuminating below us the flat surface of the marsh which stretched away to the east and south as far as the eye could see.

So flat was it that we immediately made out the silhouettes of two mules tethered below us a quarter of a mile away.

Something about the attitude of these mules arrested our attention, and, gazing upon them through our field-glasses we beheld Professor Bottomly.

That resourceful lady had mounted a pneumatic hammock upon the two mules, their saddles had sockets to fit the legs of the galvanized iron tripod.

No matter in which way the mules turned, sliding swivels on the hollow steel frames regulated the hammock slung between them. It was an infernal invention.

There lay Jane Bottomly asleep, her black hair drying over the hammock's edge, gilded to a peroxide lustre by the rays of the rising sun.

I gazed upon her with a sort of ferocious pity. Her professional days were numbered. I also had her number!

"How majestically she slumbers," whispered Dr. Delmour to me, "dreaming, doubtless, of her approaching triumph."

Dr. Fooss and Professor Lezard, driving the pack-mules ahead of them, were already riding out across the marsh.

"Daisy," I said, leaning from my saddle and taking one of her gloved hands into mine, "the time has come for me to disillusion you. There are no mammoths in that mud down there."

She looked at me in blue-eyed amazement.

"You are mistaken," she said; "Professor Bottomly is celebrated for the absolute and painstaking accuracy of her deductions and the boldness and the imagination of her scientific investigations. She is the most cautious scientist in America; she would never announce such a discovery to the newspapers unless she were perfectly certain of its truth."

I was sorry for this young girl. I pressed her hand because I was sorry for her. After a few moments of deepest thought I felt so sorry for her that I kissed her.

"You mustn't," said Dr. Delmour, blushing.

The things we mustn't do are so many that I can't always remember all of them.

"Daisy," I said, "shall we pledge ourselves to each other for eternity—here in the presence of this immemorial glacier which moves a thousand inches a year—I mean an inch every thousand years—here in these awful solitudes where incalculable calculations could not enlighten us concerning the number of cubic tons of mud in that marsh—here in the presence of these innocent mules—"

"Oh, look!" exclaimed Dr. Delmour, lifting her flushed cheek from my shoulder. "There is a man in the hammock with Professor Bottomly!"

I levelled my field-glasses incredulously. Good Heavens! There was a man there. He was sitting on the edge of the hammock in a dejected attitude, his booted legs dangling.

And, as I gazed, I saw the arm of Professor Bottomly raised as though groping instinctively for something in her slumber—saw her fingers close upon the blue-flannel shirt of her companion, saw his timid futile attempts to elude her, saw him inexorably hauled back and his head forcibly pillowed upon her ample chest.

"Daisy!" I faltered, "what does yonder scene of presumable domesticity mean?"

"I—I haven't the faintest idea!" she stammered.

"Is that lady married! Or is this revelry?" I asked, sternly.

"She wasn't married when she sailed from N-New-York," faltered Dr. Delmour.

We rode forward in pained silence, spurring on until we caught up with Lezard and Fooss and the pack-mules; then we all pressed ahead, a prey, now, to the deepest moral anxiety and agitation.

The splashing of our mule's feet on the partly melted surface of the mud aroused the man as we rode up and he scrambled madly to get out of the hammock as soon as he saw us.

A detaining feminine hand reached mechanically for his collar, groped aimlessly for a moment, and fell across the hammock's edge. Evidently its owner was too sleepy for effort.

Meanwhile the man who had floundered free from the hammock, leaped overboard and came hopping stiffly over the slush toward us like a badly-winged snipe.

"Who are you?" I demanded, drawing bridle so suddenly that I found myself astride of my mule's ears. Sliding back into the saddle, I repeated the challenge haughtily, inwardly cursing my horsemanship.

He stood balancing his lank six feet six of bony altitude for a few moments without replying. His large gentle eyes of baby blue were fixed on me.

"Speak!" I said. "The reputation of a lady is at stake! Who are you? We ask, before we shoot you, for purpose of future identification."

He gazed at me wildly. "I dunno who I be," he replied. "My name was James Skaw before that there lady went an' changed it on me. She says she has changed my name to hers. I dunno. All I know is I'm married."

"Married!" echoed Dr. Delmour.

He looked dully at the girl, then fixed his large mild eyes on me.

"A mission priest done it for her a month ago when we was hikin' towards Fort Carcajou. Hoon-hel are you?" he added.

I informed him with dignity; he blinked at me, at the others, at the mules. Then he said with infinite bitterness:

"You're a fine guy, ain't you, a-wishin' this here lady onto a pore pelt-hunter what ain't never done nothin' to you!"

"Who did you say I wished on you?" I demanded, bewildered.

"That there lady a-sleepin' into the nuptool hammick! You wished her onto me—yaas you did! Whatnhel have I done to you, hey?"

We were dumb. He shoved his hand into his pocket, produced a slug of twist, slowly gnawed off a portion, and buried the remains in his vast jaw.

"All I done to you," he said, "was to write you them letters sayin's as how I found a lot of ellerphants into the mud.

"What you done to me was to send that there lady here. Was that gratitood? Man to man I ask you?"

A loud snore from the hammock startled us all. James Skaw twisted his neck turkey-like, and looked warily at the hammock, then turning toward me:

"Aw," he said, "she don't never wake up till I have breakfast ready."

"James Skaw," I said, "tell me what has happened. On my word of honor I don't know."

He regarded me with lack-lustre eyes.

"I was a-settin' onto a bowlder," said he, "a-fig-urin' out whether you was a-comin' or not, when that there lady rides up with her led-mule a trailin'.

"Sez she: 'Are you James Skaw?'

"Yes, marm,' sez I, kinder scared an' puzzled.

"'Where is them ellerphants?' sez she, reachin' down from her saddle an' takin' me by the shirt collar, an' beatin' me with her umbrella.

"Sez I, 'I have wrote to a certain gent that I would show him them ellerphants for a price. Bein' strictly hones' I can't show 'em to no one else until I hear from him.'

"With that she continood to argoo the case with her umbrella, never lettin' go of my shirt collar. Sir, she argood until dinner time, an' then she resoomed the debate until I fell asleep. The last I knowed she was still conversin'.

"An' so it went next day, all day long, an' the next day. I couldn't stand it no longer so I started for Fort Carcajau. But she bein' onto a mule, run me down easy, an' kep' beside me conversin' volooble.

"Sir, do you know what it is to listen to umbrella argooment every day, all day long, from sun-up to night-fall? An' then some more?

"I was loony, I tell you, when we met the mission priest. 'Marry me,' sez she, 'or I'll talk you to death!' I didn't realise what she was sayin' an' what I answered. But them words I uttered done the job, it seems.

"We camped there an' slep' for two days without wakin.' When I waked up I was convalescent.

"She was good to me. She made soup an' she wrapped blankets onto me an' she didn't talk no more until I was well enough to endoor it.

"An' by'm'by she brooke the nooze to me that we was married an' that she had went as far as to marry me in the sacred cause of science because man an' wife is one, an' what I knowed about them ellerphants she now had a right to know.

"Sir, she had put one over on me. So bein' strickly hones' I had to show her where them ellerphants lay froze up under the marsh."

V

Where the ambition of this infatuated woman had led her appalled us all. The personal sacrifice she had made in the name of science awed us.

Still when I remembered that detaining arm sleepily lifted from the nuptual hammock, I was not so certain concerning her continued martyrdom.

I cast an involuntary glance of critical appraisal upon James Skaw. He had the golden hair and beard of the early Christian martyr. His features were classically regular; he stood six feet six; he was lean because fit, sound as a hound's tooth, and really a superb specimen of masculine health.

Curry him and trim him and clothe him in evening dress and his physical appearance would make a sensation at the Court of St. James. Only his English required manicuring.

The longer I looked at him the better I comprehended that detaining hand from the hammock. Fabas indulcet fames.

Then, with a shock, it rushed over me that there evidently had been some ground for this man's letters to me concerning a herd of frozen mammoths.

Professor Bottomly had not only married him to obtain the information but here she was still camping on the marsh!

"James Skaw," I said, tremulously, "where are those mammoths?"

He looked at me, then made a vague gesture:

"Under the mud—everywhere—all around us."

"Has she seen them?"

"Yes, I showed her about a hundred. There's one under you. Look! you can see him through the slush."

"Ach Gott!" burst from Dr. Fooss, and he tottered in his saddle. Lezard, frightfully pale, passed a shaking hand over his brow. As for me my hair became dank with misery, for there directly under my feet, the vast hairy bulk of a mammoth lay dimly visible through the muddy ice.

What I had done to myself when I was planning to do Professor Bottomly suddenly burst upon me in all its hideous proportions. Fame, the plaudits of the world, the highest scientific honours—all these in my effort to annihilate her, I had deliberately thrust upon this woman to my own everlasting detriment and disgrace.

A sort of howl escaped from Dr. Fooss, who had dismounted and who had been scratching in the slush with his feet like a hen.

79

For already this slight gallinaceous effort of his had laid bare a hairy section of frozen mammoth.

Lezard, weeping bitterly, squatted beside him clawing at the thin skin of ice with a pick-axe.

It seemed more than I could bear and I flung myself from my mule and seizing a spade, fell violently to work, the tears of rage and mortification coursing down my cheeks.

"Hurrah!" cried Dr. Delmour, excitedly, scrambling down from her mule and lifting a box of dynamite from her saddle-bags.

Transfigured with enthusiasm she seized a crowbar, traced in the slush the huge outlines of the buried beast, then, measuring with practiced eye the irregular zone of cleavage, she marked out a vast oval, dug holes along it with her bar, dropped into each hole a stick of dynamite, got out the batteries and wires, attached the fuses, covered each charge, and retired on a run toward the moraine, unreeling wire as she sped upward among the bowlders.

Half frantic with grief and half mad with the excitement of the moment we still had sense enough to shoulder our tools and drive our mules back across the moraine.

Only the mule-hammock in which reposed Professor Bottomly remained on the marsh. For one horrid instant temptation assailed me to press the button before James Skaw could lead the hammock-mules up to the moraine. It was my closest approach to crime.

With a shudder I viewed the approach of the mules. James Skaw led them by the head; the hammock on its bar and swivels swung gently between them; Professor Bottomly slept, lulled, no doubt, to deeper slumber by the gently swaying hammock.

When the hammock came up, one by one we gazed upon its unconscious occupant.

And, even amid dark and revengeful thoughts, amid a mental chaos of grief and fury and frantic self-reproach, I had to admit to myself that Jane Bottomly was a fine figure of a woman, and good-looking, too, and that her hair was all her own and almost magnificent at that.

With a modiste to advise her, a maid to dress her, I myself might have—but let that pass. Only as I gazed upon her fresh complexion and the softly parted red lips of Professor Bottomly, and as I noted the beautiful white throat and prettily shaped hands, a newer, bitterer, and more overwhelming despair seized me; and I realized now that perhaps I had thrown away more than fame, honours, applause; I had perhaps thrown away love!

At that moment Professor Bottomly awoke. For a moment her lilac-tinted eyes had a dazed expression, then they widened, and she lay very quietly looking from one to another of us, cradled in the golden glory of her hair, perfectly mistress of herself, and her mind as clear as a bell.

"Well," she said, "so you have arrived at last." And to Dr. Delmour she smilingly extended a cool, fresh hand.

"Have you met my husband?" she inquired.

We admitted that we had.

"James!" she called.

At the sound of her voice James Skaw hopped nimbly to do her bidding. A tender smile came into her face as she gazed upon her husband. She made no explanation concerning him, no apology for him. And, watching her, it slowly filtered into my mind that she liked him.

With one hand in her husband's and one on Dr. Delmour's arm she listened to Daisy's account of what we were about to do to the imbedded mammoth, and nodded approval.

James Skaw turned the mules so that she might watch the explosion. She twisted up her hair, then sat up in her hammock; Daisy Delmour pressed the electric button; there came a deep jarring sound, a vast upheaval, and up out of the mud rose five or six dozen mammoths and toppled gently over upon the surface of the ice.

Miserable as we were at such an astonishing spectacle we raised a tragic cheer as Professor Bottomly sprang out of her hammock and, telling Dr. Delmour to get a camera, seized her husband and sped down to where one of the great, hairy frozen beasts lay on the ice in full sunshine.

And then we tasted the last drop of gall which our over-slopping cup of bitterness held for us; Professor Bottomly climbed up the sides of the frozen mammoth, dragging her husband with her, and stood there waving a little American flag while Dr. Delmour used up every film in the camera to record the scientific triumph of the ages.

Almost idiotic with the shock of my great grief I reeled and tottered away among the bowlders. Fooss came to find me; and when he found me he kicked me violently for some time. "Esel dumkopf!" he said.

When he was tired Lezard came and fell upon me, showering me with kicks and anathema.

When he went away I beat my head with my fists for a while. Every little helped.

After a time I smelled cooking, and presently Dr. Delmour came to where I sat huddled up miserably in the sun behind the bowlder.

"Luncheon is ready," she said.

I groaned.

"Don't you feel well?"

I said that I did not.

She lingered apparently with the idea of cheering me up. "It's been such fun," she said. "Professor Lezard and I have already located over a hundred and fifty mammoths within a short distance of here, and apparently there are hundreds, if not thousands, more in the vicinity. The ivory alone is worth over a million dollars. Isn't it wonderful!"

She laughed excitedly and danced away to join the others. Then, out of the black depth of my misery a feeble gleam illuminated the Stygian obscurity. There was one way left to stay my approaching downfall—only one. Professor Bottomly meant to get rid of me, "for the good of the Bronx," but there remained a way to ward off impending disaster. And though I had lost the opportunity of my life by disbelieving the simple honesty of James Skaw,—and though the honors and emoluments and applause which ought to have been mine were destined for this determined woman, still, if I kept my head, I should be able to hold my job at the Bronx.

Dr. Delmour was immovable in the good graces of Professor Bottomly; and the only way for me to retain my position was to marry her.

The thought comforted me. After a while I felt well enough to arise and partake of some luncheon.

They were all seated around the campfire when I approached. I was welcomed politely, inquiries concerning my health were offered; but the coldly malevolent glare of Dr. Fooss and the calm contempt in Lezard's gaze chilled me; and I squatted down by Daisy Delmour and accepted a dish of soup from her in mortified silence.

Professor Bottomly and James Skaw were feasting connubially side by side, and she was selecting titbits for him which he dutifully swallowed, his large mild eyes gazing at vacancy in a gentle, surprised sort of way as he gulped down what she offered him.

Neither of them paid any attention to anybody else.

Fooss gobbled his lunch in a sort of raging silence; Lezard, on the other side of Dr. Delmour, conversed with her continually in undertones.

After a while his persistent murmuring began to make me uneasy, even suspicious, and I glared at him sideways.

Daisy Delmour, catching my eye, blushed, hesitated, then leaning over toward me with delightful confusion she whispered:

"I know that you will be glad to hear that I have just promised to marry your closest friend, Professor Lezard—"

"What!" I shouted with all my might, "have you put one over on me, too?"

Lezard and Fooss seized me, for I had risen and was jumping up and down and splashing them with soup.

"Everybody has put one over on me!" I shrieked. "Everybody! Now I'm going to put one over on myself!"

And I lifted my plate of soup and reversed it on my head.

They told me later that I screamed for half an hour before I swooned.

Afterward, my intellect being impaired, instead of being dismissed from my department, I was promoted to the position which I now hold as President Emeritus of the Consolidated Art Museums and Zoölogical Gardens of the City of New York.

I have easy hours, little to do, and twenty ornamental stenographers and typewriters engaged upon my memoirs which I dictate when I feel like it, steeped in the aroma of the most inexpensive cigar I can buy at the Rolling Stone Inn.

There is one typist in particular—but let that pass.

Vir sapit qui pauca loquitor.

UN PEU D'AMOUR

When I returned to the plateau from my investigation of the crater, I realized that I had descended the grassy pit as far as any human being could descend. No living creature could pass that barrier of flame and vapour. Of that I was convinced.

Now, not only the crater but its steaming effluvia was utterly unlike anything I had ever before beheld. There was no trace of lava to be seen, or of pumice, ashes, or of volcanic rejecta in any form whatever. There were no sulphuric odours, no pungent fumes, nothing to teach the olfactory nerves what might be the nature of the silvery steam rising from the crater incessantly in a vast circle, ringing its circumference halfway down the slope.

Under this thin curtain of steam a ring of pale yellow flames played and sparkled, completely encircling the slope.

The crater was about half a mile deep; the sides sloped gently to the bottom.

But the odd feature of the entire phenomenon was this: the bottom of the crater seemed to be entirely free from fire and vapour. It was disk-shaped, sandy, and flat, about a quarter of a mile in diameter. Through my field-glasses I could see patches of grass and wild flowers growing in the sand here and there, and the sparkle of water, and a crow or two, feeding and walking about.

I looked at the girl who was standing beside me, then cast a glance around at the very unusual landscape.

We were standing on the summit of a mountain some two thousand feet high, looking into a cup-shaped depression or crater, on the edges of which we stood.

This low, flat-topped mountain, as I say, was grassy and quite treeless, although it rose like a truncated sugar-cone out of a wilderness of trees which stretched for miles below us, north, south, east, and west, bordered on the horizon by towering blue mountains, their distant ranges enclosing the forests as in a vast amphitheatre.

From the centre of this enormous green floor of foliage rose our grassy hill, and it appeared to be the only irregularity which broke the level wilderness as far as the base of the dim blue ranges encircling the horizon.

Except for the log bungalow of Mr. Blythe on the eastern edge of this grassy plateau, there was not a human habitation in sight, nor a trace of man's devastating presence in the wilderness around us.

Again I looked questioningly at the girl beside me and she looked back at me rather seriously.

"Shall we seat ourselves here in the sun?" she asked.

I nodded.

Very gravely we settled down side by side on the thick green grass.

"Now," she said, "I shall tell you why I wrote you to come out here. Shall I?"

"By all means, Miss Blythe."

Sitting cross-legged, she gathered her ankles into her hands, settling herself as snugly on the grass as a bird settles on its nest.

"The phenomena of nature," she said, "have always interested me intensely, not only from the artistic angle but from the scientific point of view.

"It is different with father. He is a painter; he cares only for the artistic aspects of nature. Phenomena of a scientific nature bore him. Also, you may have noticed that he is of a—a slightly impatient disposition."

I had noticed it. He had been anything but civil to me when I arrived the night before, after a five-hundred mile trip on a mule, from the nearest railroad—a journey performed entirely alone and by compass, there being no trail after the first fifty miles.

To characterize Blythe as slightly impatient was letting him down easy. He was a selfish, bad-tempered old pig.

"Yes," I said, answering her, "I did notice a negligible trace of impatience about your father."

She flushed.

"You see I did not inform my father that I had written to you. He doesn't like strangers; he doesn't like scientists. I did not dare tell him that I had asked you to come out here. It was entirely my own idea. I felt that I must write you because I am positive that what is happening in this wilderness is of vital scientific importance."

"How did you get a letter out of this distant and desolate place?" I asked.

"Every two months the storekeeper at Windflower Station sends in a man and a string of mules with staples for us. The man takes our further orders and our letters back to civilization."

I nodded.

"He took my letter to you—among one or two others I sent——"

A charming colour came into her cheeks. She was really extremely pretty. I liked that girl. When a girl blushes when she speaks to a man he immediately accepts her heightened colour as a personal tribute. This is not vanity: it is merely a proper sense of personal worthiness.

She said thoughtfully:

"The mail bag which that man brought to us last week contained a letter which, had I received it earlier, would have made my invitation to you unnecessary. I'm sorry I disturbed you."

"I am not," said I, looking into her beautiful eyes.

I twisted my mustache into two attractive points, shot my cuffs, and glanced at her again, receptively.

She had a far-away expression in her eyes. I straightened my necktie. A man, without being vain, ought to be conscious of his own worth.

"And now," she continued, "I am going to tell you the various reasons why I asked so celebrated a scientist as yourself to come here."

I thanked her for her encomium.

"Ever since my father retired from Boston to purchase this hill and the wilderness surrounding it," she went on, "ever since he came here to live a hermit's life—a life devoted solely to painting landscapes—I also have lived here all alone with him.

"That is three years, now. And from the very beginning—from the very first day of our arrival, somehow or other I was conscious that there was something abnormal about this corner of the world."

She bent forward, lowering her voice a trifle:

"Have you noticed," she asked, "that so many things seem to be circular out here?"

"Circular?" I repeated, surprised.

"Yes. That crater is circular; so is the bottom of it; so is this plateau, and the hill; and the forests surrounding us; and the mountain ranges on the horizon."

"But all this is natural."

"Perhaps. But in those woods, down there, there are, here and there, great circles of crumbling soil—perfect circles a mile in diameter."

"Mounds built by prehistoric man, no doubt."

She shook her head:

"These are not prehistoric mounds."

"Why not?"

"Because they have been freshly made."

"How do you know?"

"The earth is freshly upheaved; great trees, partly uprooted, slant at every angle from the sides of the enormous piles of newly upturned earth; sand and stones are still sliding from the raw ridges."

She leaned nearer and dropped her voice still lower:

"More than that," she said, "my father and I both have seen one of these huge circles in the making!"

"What!" I exclaimed, incredulously.

"It is true. We have seen several. And it enrages father."

"Enrages?"

"Yes, because it upsets the trees where he is painting landscapes, and tilts them in every direction. Which, of course, ruins his picture; and he is obliged to start another, which vexes him dreadfully."

I think I must have gaped at her in sheer astonishment.

"But there is something more singular than that for you to investigate," she said calmly. "Look down at that circle of steam which makes a perfect ring around the bowl of the crater, halfway down. Do you see the flicker of fire under the vapour?"

"Yes."

She leaned so near and spoke in such a low voice that her fragrant breath fell upon my cheek:

"In the fire, under the vapours, there are little animals."

"What!!"

"Little beasts live in the fire—slim, furry creatures, smaller than a weasel. I've seen them peep out of the fire and scurry back into it.... Now are you sorry that I wrote you to come? And will you forgive me for bringing you out here?"

An indescribable excitement seized me, endowing me with a fluency and eloquence unusual:

"I thank you from the bottom of my heart!" I cried; "—from the depths of a heart the emotions of which are entirely and exclusively of scientific origin!"

In the impulse of the moment I held out my hand; she laid hers in it with charming diffidence.

"Yours is the discovery," I said. "Yours shall be the glory. Fame shall crown you; and perhaps if there remains any reflected light in the form of a by-product, some modest and negligible little ray may chance to illuminate me."

Surprised and deeply moved by my eloquence, I bent over her hand and saluted it with my lips.

She thanked me. Her pretty face was rosy.

It appeared that she had three cows to milk, new-laid eggs to gather, and the construction of some fresh butter to be accomplished.

At the bars of the grassy pasture slope she dropped me a

curtsey, declining very shyly to let me carry her lacteal paraphernalia.

So I continued on to the bungalow garden, where Blythe sat on a camp stool under a green umbrella, painting a picture of something or other.

"Mr. Blythe!" I cried, striving to subdue my enthusiasm. "The eyes of the scientific world are now open upon this house! The searchlight of Fame is about to be turned upon you—"

"I prefer privacy," he interrupted. "That's why I came here. I'll be obliged if you'll turn off that searchlight."

"But, my dear Mr. Blythe—"

"I want to be let alone," he repeated irritably. "I came out here to paint and to enjoy privately my own paintings."

If what stood on his easel was a sample of his pictures, nobody was likely to share his enjoyment.

"Your work," said I, politely, "is—is——"

"Is what!" he snapped. "What is it—if you think you know?"

"It is entirely, so to speak, per se—by itself—"

"What the devil do you mean by that?"

I looked at his picture, appalled. The entire canvas was one monotonous vermillion conflagration. I examined it with my head on one side, then on the other side; I made a funnel with both hands and peered intently through it at the picture. A menacing murmuring sound came from him.

"Satisfying—exquisitely satisfying," I concluded. "I have often seen such sunsets—"

"What!"

"I mean such prairie fires—"

"Damnation!" he exclaimed. "I'm painting a bowl of nasturtiums!"

"I was speaking purely in metaphor," said I with a sickly smile. "To me a nasturtium by the river brink is more than a simple flower. It is a broader, grander, more magnificent, more stupendous symbol. It may mean anything, everything—such as sunsets and conflagrations and Götterdämmerungs! Or—" and my voice was subtly modulated to an appealing and persuasive softness—"it may mean nothing at all—chaos, void, vacuum, negation, the exquisite annihilation of what has never even existed."

He glared at me over his shoulder. If he was infected by Cubist tendencies he evidently had not understood what I said.

"If you won't talk about my pictures I don't mind your investigating this district," he grunted, dabbing at his palette and plastering a wad of vermilion upon his canvas; "but I object to any public invasion of my artistic privacy until I am ready for it."

"When will that be?"

He pointed with one vermilion-soaked brush toward a long, low, log building.

"In that structure," he said, "are packed one thousand and ninety-five paintings—all signed by me. I have executed one or two every day since I came here. When I have painted exactly ten thousand pictures, no more, no less, I shall erect here a gallery large enough to contain them all.

"Only real lovers of art will ever come here to study them. It is five hundred miles from the railroad. Therefore, I shall never have to endure the praises of the dilettante, the patronage of the idler, the vapid rhapsodies of the vulgar. Only those who understand will care to make the pilgrimage."

He waved his brushes at me:

"The conservation of national resources is all well enough—the setting aside of timber reserves, game preserves, bird refuges, all these projects are very good in a way. But I have dedicated this wilderness as a last and only refuge in all the world for true Art! Because true Art, except for my pictures, is, I believe, now practically extinct!... You're in my way. Would you mind getting out?"

I had sidled around between him and his bowl of nasturtiums, and I hastily stepped aside. He squinted at the flowers, mixed up a flamboyant mess of colour on his palette, and daubed away with unfeigned satisfaction, no longer noticing me until I started to go. Then:

"What is it you're here for, anyway?" he demanded abruptly. I said with dignity:

"I am here to investigate those huge rings of earth thrown up in the forest as by a gigantic mole." He continued to paint for a few moments:

"Well, go and investigate 'em," he snapped. "I'm not infatuated with your society."

"What do you think they are?" I asked, mildly ignoring his wretched manners.

"I don't know and I don't care, except, that sometimes when I begin to paint several trees, the very trees I'm painting are suddenly heaved up and tilted in every direction, and all my work goes for nothing. That makes me mad! Otherwise, the matter has no interest for me."

"But what in the world could cause—"

"I don't know and I don't care!" he shouted, waving palette and brushes angrily. "Maybe it's an army of moles working all together under the ground; maybe it's some species of circular earthquake. I don't know! I don't care! But it annoys me. And if you can devise any scientific means to stop it, I'll be much obliged to you. Otherwise, to be perfectly frank, you bore me."

"The mission of Science," said I solemnly, "is to alleviate the inconveniences of mundane existence. Science, therefore, shall extend a helping hand to her frailer sister, Art—"

"Science can't patronize Art while I'm around!" he retorted. "I won't have it!"

"But, my dear Mr. Blythe—"

"I won't dispute with you, either! I don't like to dispute!" he shouted. "Don't try to make me. Don't attempt to inveigle me into discussion! I know all I want to know. I don't want to know anything you want me to know, either!"

I looked at the old pig in haughty silence, nauseated by his conceit.

After he had plastered a few more tubes of vermilion over his canvas he quieted down, and presently gave me an oblique glance over his shoulder.

"Well," he said, "what else are you intending to investigate?"

"Those little animals that live in the crater fires," I said bluntly.

"Yes," he nodded, indifferently, "there are creatures which live somewhere in the fires of that crater."

"Do you realize what an astounding statement you are making?" I asked.

"It doesn't astound me. What do I care whether it astounds you or anybody else? Nothing interests me except Art."

"But—"

"I tell you nothing interests me except Art!" he yelled. "Don't dispute it! Don't answer me! Don't irritate me! I don't care whether anything lives in the fire or not! Let it live there!"

"But have you actually seen live creatures in the flames?"

"Plenty! Plenty! What of it? What about it? Let 'em live there, for all I care. I've painted pictures of 'em, too. That's all that interests me."

"What do they look like, Mr. Blythe?"

"Look like? I don't know! They look like weasels or rats or bats or cats or—stop asking me questions! It irritates me! It depresses me! Don't ask any more! Why don't you go in to lunch? And—tell my daughter to bring me a bowl of salad out here. I've no time to stuff myself. Some people have. I haven't. You'd better go in to lunch.... And tell my daughter to bring me seven tubes of Chinese vermilion with my salad!"

"You don't mean to mix—" I began, then checked myself before his fury.

"I'd rather eat vermilion paint on my salad than sit here talking to you!" he shouted.

I cast a pitying glance at this impossible man, and went into the house. After all, he was her father. I had to endure him.

After Miss Blythe had carried to her father a large bucket of lettuce leaves, she returned to the veranda of the bungalow.

A delightful luncheon awaited us; I seated her, then took the chair opposite.

A delicious omelette, fresh biscuit, salad, and strawberry preserves, and a tall tumbler of iced tea imbued me with a sort of mild exhilaration.

Out of the corner of my eye I could see Blythe down in the garden, munching his lettuce leaves like an ill-tempered rabbit, and daubing away at his picture while he munched.

"Your father," said I politely, "is something of a genius."

"I am so glad you think so," she said gratefully. "But don't tell him so. He has been surfeited with praise in Boston. That is why we came out here."

"Art," said I, "is like science, or tobacco, or tooth-wash. Every man to his own brand. Personally, I don't care for his kind. But who can say which is the best kind of anything? Only the consumer. Your father is his own consumer. He is the best judge of what he likes. And that is the only true test of art, or anything else."

"How delightfully you reason!" she said. "How logically, how generously!"

"Reason is the handmaid of Science, Miss Blythe."

She seemed to understand me. Her quick intelligence surprised me, because I myself was not perfectly sure whether I had emitted piffle or an epigram.

As we ate our strawberry preserves we discussed ways and means of capturing a specimen of the little fire creatures which, as she explained, so frequently peeped out at her from the crater fires, and, at her slightest movement, scurried back again into the flames. Of course I believed that this was only her imagination. Yet, for years I had entertained a theory that fire supported certain unknown forms of life.

"I have long believed," said I, "that fire is inhabited by living organisms which require the elements and temperature of active combustion for their existence—microörganisms, but not," I added smilingly, "any higher type of life."

"In the fireplace," she ventured diffidently, "I sometimes see curious things—dragons and snakes and creatures of grotesque and peculiar shapes."

I smiled indulgently, charmed by this innocently offered

contribution to science. Then she rose, and I rose and took her hand in mine, and we wandered over the grass toward the crater, while I explained to her the difference between what we imagine we see in the glowing coals of a grate fire and my own theory that fire is the abode of living animalculae.

On the grassy edge of the crater we paused and looked down the slope, where the circle of steam rose, partly veiling the pale flash of fire underneath.

"How near can we go?" I inquired.

"Quite near. Come; I'll guide you."

Leading me by the hand, she stepped over the brink and we began to descend the easy grass slope together.

There was no difficulty about it at all. Down we went, nearer and nearer to the wall of steam, until at last, when but fifteen feet away from it, I felt the heat from the flames which sparkled below the wall of vapour.

Here we seated ourselves upon the grass, and I knitted my brows and fixed my eyes upon this curious phenomenon, striving to discover some reason for it.

Except for the vapour and the fires, there was nothing whatever volcanic about this spectacle, or in the surroundings.

From where I sat I could see that the bed of fire which encircled the crater; and the wall of vapour which crowned the flames, were about three hundred feet wide. Of course this barrier was absolutely impassable. There was no way of getting through it into the bottom of the crater.

A slight pressure from Miss Blythe's fingers engaged my attention; I turned toward her, and she said:

"There is one more thing about which I have not told you. I feel a little guilty, because that is the real reason I asked you to come here."

"What is it?"

"I think there are emeralds on the floor of that crater."

"Emeralds!"

"I think so." She felt in the ruffled pocket of her apron, drew out a fragment of mineral, and passed it to me.

I screwed a jeweler's glass into my eye and examined it in astonished silence. It was an emerald; a fine, large, immensely valuable stone, if my experience counted for anything. One side of it was thickly coated with vermilion paint.

"Where did this come from?" I asked in an agitated voice.

"From the floor of the crater. Is it really an emerald?"

I lifted my head and stared at the girl incredulously.

"It happened this way," she said excitedly. "Father was painting a picture up there by the edge of the crater. He left his palette on the grass to go to the bungalow for some more tubes of colour. While he was in the house, hunting for the colours which he wanted, I stepped out on the veranda, and I saw some crows alight near the palette and begin to stalk about in the grass. One bird walked right over his wet palette; I stepped out and waved my sun-bonnet to frighten him off, but he had both feet in a sticky mass of Chinese vermilion, and for a moment was unable to free himself.

"I almost caught him, but he flapped away over the edge of the crater, high above the wall of vapour, sailed down onto the crater floor, and alighted.

"But his feet bothered him; he kept hopping about on the bottom of the crater, half running, half flying; and finally he took wing and rose up over the hill.

"As he flew above me, and while I was looking up at his vermilion feet, something dropped from his claws and nearly struck me. It was that emerald."

When I had recovered sufficient composure to speak steadily, I took her beautiful little hand in mine.

"This," said I, "is the most exciting locality I have ever visited for purposes of scientific research. Within this crater may lie millions of value in emeralds. You are probably, today, the wealthiest heiress upon the face of the globe!"

I gave her a winning glance. She smiled, shyly, and blushingly withdrew her hand.

For several exquisite minutes I sat there beside her in a sort of heavenly trance. How beautiful she was! How engaging—how sweet—how modestly appreciative of the man beside her, who had little beside his scientific learning, his fame, and a kind heart to appeal to such youth and loveliness as hers!

There was something about her that delicately appealed to me. Sometimes I pondered what this might be; sometimes I wondered how many emeralds lay on that floor of sandy gravel below us.

Yes, I loved her. I realised it now. I could even endure her father for her sake. I should make a good husband. I was quite certain of that.

I turned and gazed upon her, meltingly. But I did not wish to startle her, so I remained silent, permitting the chaste language of my eyes to interpret for her what my lips had not yet murmured. It was a brief but beautiful moment in my life.

"The way to do," said I, "is to trap several dozen crows, smear their feet with glue, tie a ball of Indian twine to the ankle of every bird, then liberate them. Some are certain to fly into the crater and try to scrape the glue off in the sand. Then," I added, triumphantly, "all we have to do is to haul in our birds and detach the wealth of Midas from their sticky claws!"

"That is an excellent suggestion," she said gratefully, "but I can do that after you have gone. All I wanted you to tell me was whether the stone is a genuine emerald."

I gazed at her blankly.

"You are here for purposes of scientific investigation," she added, sweetly. "I should not think of taking your time for the mere sake of accumulating wealth for my father and me."

There didn't seem to be anything for me to say at that moment. Chilled, I gazed at the flashing ring of fire.

And, as I gazed, suddenly I became aware of a little, pointed muzzle, two pricked-up ears, and two ruby-red eyes gazing intently out at me from the mass of flames.

The girl beside me saw it, too.

"Don't move!" she whispered. "That is one of the flame creatures. It may venture out if you keep perfectly still."

Rigid with amazement, I sat like a stone image, staring at the most astonishing sight I had ever beheld.

For several minutes the ferret-like creature never stirred from where it crouched in the crater fire; the alert head remained pointed toward us; I could even see that its thick fur must have possessed the qualities of asbestos, because here and there a hair or two glimmered incandescent; and its eyes, nose, and whiskers glowed and glowed as the flames pulsated around it.

After a long while it began to move out of the fire, slowly, cautiously, cunning eyes fixed on us—a small, slim, wiry, weasel-like creature on which the sunlight fell with a vitreous glitter as it crept forward into the grass.

Then, from the fire behind, another creature of the same sort appeared, another, others, then dozens of eager, lithe, little animals appeared everywhere from the flames and began to frisk and play and run about in the grass and nibble the fresh, green, succulent herbage with a snipping sound quite audible to us.

One came so near my feet that I could examine it minutely.

Its fur and whiskers seemed heavy and dense and like asbestos fibre, yet so fine as to appear silky. Its eyes, nose, and claws were scarlet, and seemed to possess a glassy surface.

I waited my opportunity, and when the little thing came nosing along within reach, I seized it.

Instantly it emitted a bewildering series of whistling shrieks, and twisted around to bite me. Its body was icy.

"Don't let it bite!" cried the girl. "Be careful, Mr. Smith!"

But its jaws were toothless; only soft, cold gums pinched me, and I held it twisting and writhing, while the icy temperature of its body began to benumb my fingers and creep up my wrist, paralyzing my arm; and its incessant and piercing shrieks deafened me.

In vain I transferred it to the other hand, and then passed it from one hand to the other, as one shifts a lump of ice or a hot potato, in an attempt to endure the temperature: it shrieked and squirmed and doubled, and finally wriggled out of my stiffened and useless hands, and scuttled away into the fire.

It was an overwhelming disappointment. For a moment it seemed unendurable.

"Never mind," I said, huskily, "if I caught one in my hands, I can surely catch another in a trap."

"I am so sorry for your disappointment," she said, pitifully.

"Do you care, Miss Blythe?" I asked.

She blushed.

"Of course I care," she murmured.

My hands were too badly frost-nipped to become eloquent. I merely sighed and thrust them into my pockets. Even my arm was too stiff to encircle her shapeful waist. Devotion to Science had temporarily crippled me. Love must wait. But, as we ascended the grassy slope together, I promised myself that I would make her a good husband, and that I should spend at least part of every day of my life in trapping crows and smearing their claws with glue.

That evening I was seated on the veranda beside Wilna—Miss Blythe's name was Wilna—and what with gazing at her and fitting together some of the folding box-traps which I always carried with me—and what with trying to realise the pecuniary magnificence of our future existence together, I was exceedingly busy when Blythe came in to display, as I supposed, his most recent daub to me.

The canvas he carried presented a series of crimson speckles, out of which burst an eruption of green streaks—and it made me think of stepping on a caterpillar.

My instinct was to placate this impossible man. He was her father. I meant to honour him if I had to assault him to do it.

"Supremely satisfying!" I nodded, chary of naming the subject. "It is a stride beyond the art of the future: it is a flying leap out of the Not Yet into the Possibly Perhaps! I thank you for enlightening me, Mr. Blythe. I am your debtor."

He fairly snarled at me:

"What are you talking about!" he demanded.

I remained modestly mute.

To Wilna he said, pointing passionately at his canvas:

"The crows have been walking all over it again! I'm going to paint in the woods after this, earthquakes or no earthquakes. Have the trees been heaved up anywhere recently?"

"Not since last week," she said, soothingly. "It usually happens after a rain."

"I think I'll risk it then—although it did rain early this morning. I'll do a moonlight down there this evening." And, turning to me: "If you know as much about science as you do about art you won't have to remain here long—I trust."

"What?" said I, very red.

He laughed a highly disagreeable laugh, and marched into the house. Presently he bawled for dinner, and Wilna went away. For her sake I had remained calm and dignified, but presently I went out and kicked up the turf two or three times; and, having foozled my wrath, I went back to dinner, realising that I might as well begin to accustom myself to my future father-in-law.

It seemed that he had a mania for prunes, and that's all he permitted anybody to have for dinner.

Disgusted, I attempted to swallow the loathly stewed fruit, watching Blythe askance as he hurriedly stuffed himself, using a tablespoon, with every symptom of relish.

"Now," he cried, shoving back his chair, "I'm going to paint a moonlight by moonlight. Wilna, if Billy arrives, make him comfortable, and tell him I'll return by midnight." And without taking the trouble to notice me at all, he strode away toward the veranda, chewing vigorously upon his last prune.

"Your father," said I, "is eccentric. Genius usually is. But he is a most interesting and estimable man. I revere him."

"It is kind of you to say so," said the girl, in a low voice.

I thought deeply for a few moments, then:

"Who is 'Billy?'" I inquired, casually.

I couldn't tell whether it was a sudden gleam of sunset light on her face, or whether she blushed.

"Billy," she said softly, "is a friend of father's. His name is William Green."

"Oh."

"He is coming out here to visit—father—I believe."

"Oh. An artist; and doubtless of mature years."

"He is a mineralogist by profession," she said, "—and somewhat young."

"Oh."

"Twenty-four years old," she added. Upon her pretty face was an absent expression, vaguely pleasant. Her blue eyes became dreamy and exquisitely remote.

I pondered deeply for a while:

"Wilna?" I said.

"Yes, Mr. Smith?" as though aroused from agreeable meditation.

But I didn't know exactly what to say, and I remained uneasily silent, thinking about that man Green and his twenty-four years, and his profession, and the bottom of the crater, and Wilna—and striving to satisfy myself that there was no logical connection between any of these.

"I think," said I, "that I'll take a bucket of salad to your father."

Why I should have so suddenly determined to ingratiate myself with the old grouch I scarcely understood: for the construction of a salad was my very best accomplishment.

Wilna looked at me in a peculiar manner, almost as though she were controlling a sudden and not unpleasant inward desire to laugh.

Evidently the finer and more delicate instincts of a woman were divining my motive and sympathizing with my mental and sentimental perplexity.

So when she said: "I don't think you had better go near my father," I was convinced of her gentle solicitude in my behalf.

"With a bucket of salad," I whispered softly, "much may be accomplished, Wilna." And I took her little hand and pressed it gently and respectfully. "Trust all to me," I murmured.

She stood with her head turned away from me, her slim hand resting limply in mine. From the slight tremor of her shoulders I became aware how deeply her emotion was now swaying her. Evidently she was nearly ready to become mine.

But I remained calm and alert. The time was not yet. Her father had had his prunes, in which he delighted. And when pleasantly approached with a bucket of salad he could not listen otherwise than politely to what I had to say to him. Quick action was necessary—quick but diplomatic action—in view of the imminence of this young man Green, who evidently was persona grata at the bungalow of this irritable old dodo.

Tenderly pressing the pretty hand which I held, and saluting the finger-tips with a gesture which was, perhaps, not wholly ungraceful, I stepped into the kitchen, washed out several heads of lettuce, deftly chopped up some youthful onions, constructed a seductive French dressing, and, stirring together the crisp ingredients, set the savoury masterpiece away in the ice-box, after tasting it. It was delicious enough to draw sobs from any pig.

When I went out to the veranda, Wilna had disappeared. So I unfolded and set up some more box-traps, determined to lose no time.

Sunset still lingered beyond the chain of western mountains as I went out across the grassy plateau to the cornfield.

Here I set and baited several dozen aluminium crow-traps, padding the jaws so that no injury could be done to the birds when the springs snapped on their legs.

Then I went over to the crater and descended its gentle, grassy slope. And there, all along the borders of the vapoury wall, I set box-traps for the lithe little denizens of the fire, baiting every trap with a handful of fresh, sweet clover which I had pulled up from the pasture beyond the cornfield.

My task ended, I ascended the slope again, and for a while stood there immersed in pleasurable premonitions.

Everything had been accomplished swiftly and methodically within the few hours in which I had first set eyes upon this extraordinary place—everything!—love at first sight, the delightfully lightning-like wooing and winning of an incomparable maiden and heiress; the discovery of the fire creatures; the solving of the emerald problem.

And now everything was ready, crow-traps, fire-traps, a bucket of irresistible salad for Blythe, a modest and tremulous avowal for Wilna as soon as her father tasted the salad and I had pleasantly notified him of my intentions concerning his lovely offspring.

Daylight faded from rose to lilac; already the mountains were growing fairy-like under that vague, diffuse lustre which heralds the rise of the full moon. It rose, enormous, yellow, unreal, becoming imperceptibly silvery as it climbed the sky and hung aloft like a stupendous arc-light flooding the world with a radiance so white and clear that I could very easily have written verses by it, if I wrote verses.

Down on the edge of the forest I could see Blythe on his camp-stool, madly besmearing his moonlit canvas, but I could not see Wilna anywhere. Maybe she had shyly retired somewhere by herself to think of me.

So I went back to the house, filled a bucket with my salad, and started toward the edge of the woods, singing happily as I sped on feet so light and frolicsome that they seemed to skim the ground. How wonderful is the power of love!

When I approached Blythe he heard me coming and turned around.

"What the devil do you want?" he asked with characteristic civility.

"I have brought you," said I gaily, "a bucket of salad."

"I don't want any salad!"

"W-what?"

"I never eat it at night."

I said confidently:

"Mr. Blythe, if you will taste this salad I am sure you will not regret it." And with hideous cunning I set the bucket beside him on the grass and seated myself near it. The old dodo grunted and continued to daub the canvas; but presently, as though forgetfully, and from sheer instinct, he reached down into the bucket, pulled out a leaf of lettuce, and shoved it into his mouth.

My heart leaped exultantly. I had him!

"Mr. Blythe," I began in a winningly modulated voice, and, at the same instant, he sprang from his camp-chair, his face distorted.

"There are onions in this salad!" he yelled. "What the devil do you mean! Are you trying to poison me! What are you following me about for, anyway? Why are you running about under foot every minute!"

"My dear Mr. Blythe," I protested—but he barked at me, kicked over the bucket of salad, and began to dance with rage.

"What's the matter with you, anyway!" he bawled. "Why are you trying to feed me? What do you mean by trying to be attentive to me!"

"I—I admire and revere you—"

"No you don't!" he shouted. "I don't want you to admire me! I don't desire to be revered! I don't like attention and politeness! Do you hear! It's artificial—out of date—ridiculous! The only thing that recommends a man to me is his bad manners, bad temper, and violent habits. There's some meaning to such a man, none at all to men like you!"

He ran at the salad bucket and kicked it again.

"They all fawned on me in Boston!" he panted. "They ran about under foot! They bought my pictures! And they made me sick! I came out here to be rid of 'em!"

I rose from the grass, pale and determined.

"You listen to me, you old grouch!" I hissed. "I'll go. But before I go I'll tell you why I've been civil to you. There's only one reason in the world: I want to marry your daughter! And I'm going to do it!"

I stepped nearer him, menacing him with outstretched hand:

"As for you, you pitiable old dodo, with your bad manners and your worse pictures, and your degraded mania for prunes, you are a necessary evil that's all, and I haven't the slightest respect for either you or your art!"

"Is that true?" he said in an altered voice.

"True?" I laughed bitterly. "Of course it's true, you miserable dauber!"

"D-dauber!" he stammered.

"Certainly! I said 'dauber,' and I mean it. Why, your work would shame the pictures on a child's slate!"

"Smith," he said unsteadily, "I believe I have utterly misjudged you. I believe you are a good deal of a man, after all—"

"I'm man enough," said I, fiercely, "to go back, saddle my mule, kidnap your daughter, and start for home. And I'm going to do it!"

"Wait!" he cried. "I don't want you to go. If you'll remain I'll be very glad. I'll do anything you like. I'll quarrel with you, and you can insult my pictures. It will agreeably stimulate us both. Don't go, Smith—"

"If I stay, may I marry Wilna?"

"If you ask me I won't let you!"

"Very well!" I retorted, angrily. "Then I'll marry her anyway!"

"That's the way to talk! Don't go, Smith. I'm really beginning to like you. And when Billy Green arrives you and he will have a delightfully violent scene—"

"What!"

He rubbed his hands gleefully.

"He's in love with Wilna. You and he won't get on. It is going to be very stimulating for me—I can see that! You and he are going to behave most disagreeably to each other. And I shall be exceedingly unpleasant to you both! Come, Smith, promise me that you'll stay!"

Profoundly worried, I stood staring at him in the moonlight, gnawing my mustache.

"Very well," I said, "I'll remain if—"

Something checked me, I did not quite know what for a moment. Blythe, too, was staring at me in an odd, apprehensive way. Suddenly I realised that under my feet the ground was stirring.

"Look out!" I cried; but speech froze on my lips as beneath me the solid earth began to rock and crack and billow up into a high, crumbling ridge, moving continually, as the sod cracks, heaves up, and crumbles above the subterranean progress of a mole.

Up into the air we were slowly pushed on the ever-growing ridge; and with us were carried rocks and bushes and sod, and even forest trees.

I could hear their tap-roots part with pistol-like reports; see great pines and hemlocks and oaks moving, slanting, settling, tilting crazily in every direction as they were heaved upward in this gigantic disturbance.

Blythe caught me by the arm; we clutched each other, balancing on the crest of the steadily rising mound.

"W-what is it?" he stammered. "Look! It's circular. The woods are rising in a huge circle. What's happening? Do you know?"

Over me crept a horrible certainty that something living was moving under us through the depths of the earth—something that, as it progressed, was heaping up the surface of the world above its unseen and burrowing course—something dreadful, enormous, sinister, and alive!

"Look out!" screamed Blythe; and at the same instant the crumbling summit of the ridge opened under our feet and a fissure hundreds of yards long yawned ahead of us.

And along it, shining slimily in the moonlight, a vast, viscous, ringed surface was moving, retracting, undulating, elongating, writhing, squirming, shuddering.

"It's a worm!" shrieked Blythe. "Oh, God! It's a mile long!"

As in a nightmare we clutched each other, struggling frantically to avoid the fissure; but the soft earth slid and gave way under us, and we fell heavily upon that ghastly, living surface.

Instantly a violent convulsion hurled us upward; we fell on it again, rebounding from the rubbery thing, strove to regain our feet and scramble up the edges of the fissure, strove madly while the mammoth worm slid more rapidly through the rocking forests, carrying us forward with a speed increasing.

Through the forest we tore, reeling about on the slippery back of the thing, as though riding on a plowshare, while trees clashed and tilted and fell from the enormous furrow on every side; then, suddenly out of the woods into the moonlight, far ahead of us we could see the grassy upland heave up, cake, break, and crumble above the burrowing course of the monster.

"It's making for the crater!" gasped Blythe; and horror spurred us on, and we scrambled and slipped and clawed the billowing sides of the furrow until we gained the heaving top of it.

As one runs in a bad dream, heavily, half-paralyzed, so ran Blythe and I, toiling over the undulating, tumbling upheaval until, half-fainting, we fell and rolled down the shifting slope onto solid and unvexed sod on the very edges of the crater.

Below us we saw, with sickened eyes, the entire circumference of the crater agitated, saw it rise and fall as avalanches of rock and earth slid into it, tons and thousands of tons rushing down the slope, blotting from our sight the flickering ring of flame, and extinguishing the last filmy jet of vapour.

Suddenly the entire crater caved in and filled up under my anguished eyes, quenching for all eternity the vapour wall, the fire, and burying the little denizens of the flames, and perhaps a billion dollars' worth of emeralds under as many billion tons of earth.

Quieter and quieter grew the earth as the gigantic worm bored straight down into depths immeasurable. And at last the moon shone upon a world that lay without a tremor in its milky lustre.

"I shall name it Verma gigantica," said I, with a hysterical sob; "but nobody will ever believe me when I tell this story!"

Still terribly shaken, we turned toward the house. And, as we approached the lamplit veranda, I saw a horse standing there and a young man hastily dismounting.

And then a terrible thing occurred; for, before I could even shriek, Wilna had put both arms around that young man's neck, and both of his arms were clasping her waist.

Blythe was kind to me. He took me around the back way and put me to bed.

And there I lay through the most awful night I ever experienced, listening to the piano below, where Wilna and William Green were singing, "Un Peu d'Amour."

THE EGGS OF THE SILVER MOON

In the new white marble Administration Building at Bronx Park, my private office separated the offices of Dr. Silas Quint and Professor Boomly; and it had been arranged so on purpose, because of the increasingly frequent personal misunderstanding between these two celebrated entomologists. It was very plain to me that a crisis in this quarrel was rapidly approaching.

A bitter animosity had for some months existed on both sides, born of the most intense professional jealousy. They had been friends for years. No unseemly rivalry disturbed this friendship as long as it was merely a question of collecting, preparing, and mounting for exhibition the vast numbers of butterflies and moths which haunt this insectivorous earth. Even their zeal in the eternal hunt for new and undescribed species had not made them enemies.

I am afraid that my suggestion for the construction of a great glass flying-cage for living specimens of moths and butterflies started the trouble between these hitherto godly and middle-aged men. That, and the Carnegie Educational Medal were the causes which began this deplorable affair.

Various field collectors, employed by both Quint and Boomly, were always out all over the world foraging for specimens; also, they were constantly returning with spoils from every quarter of the globe.

Now, to secure rare and beautiful living specimens of butterflies and moths for the crystal flying-cage was a serious and delicate job. Such tropical insects could not survive the journey of several months from the wilds of Australia, India, Asia, Africa, or the jungles of South America—nor could semi-tropical species endure the captivity of a few weeks or even days, when captured in the West Indies, Mexico, or Florida. Only our duller-coloured, smaller, and hardier native species tolerated capture and exhibition.

Therefore, the mode of procedure which I suggested was for our field expeditions to obtain males and females of the same species of butterfly or moth, mate them, and, as soon as any female deposited her eggs, place the tiny pearl-like eggs in cold storage to retard their hatching, which normally occurs, in the majority of species, within ten days or two weeks.

This now was the usual mode of procedure followed by the field collectors employed by Dr. Quint and Professor Boomly. And not only were the eggs of various butterflies and moths so packed for transportation, but a sufficient store of their various native food-plants was also preserved, where such food-plants could not be procured in the United States. So when the eggs arrived at Bronx Park, and were hatched there in due time, the young caterpillars had plenty of nourishment ready for them in cold storage.

Might I not, legitimately, have expected the Carnegie Educational Medal for all this? I have never received it. I say this without indignation—even without sorrow. I merely make the statement.

Yet, my system was really a very beautiful system; a tiny batch of eggs would arrive from Ceylon, or Sumatra, or Africa; when taken from cold storage and placed in the herbarium they would presently hatch; the caterpillars were fed with their accustomed food-plant—a few leaves being taken from cold storage every day for them—they would pass through their three or four moulting periods, cease feeding in due time, transform into the chrysalis stage, and finally appear in all the splendour and magnificence of butterfly or moth.

The great glass flying-cage was now alive with superb moths and butterflies, flitting, darting, fluttering among the flowering bushes or feeding along the sandy banks of the brook which flowed through the flying-cage, bordered by thickets of scented flowers. And it was like looking at a meteoric shower of winged jewels, where the huge metallic-blue Morphos from South America flapped and sailed, and the orange and gold and green Ornithoptera from Borneo pursued their majestic, bird-like flight—where big, glittering Papilios flashed through the bushes or alighted nervously to feed for a few moments on jasmine and phlox, and where the slowly flopping Heliconians winged their way amid the denser tangles of tropical vegetation.

Nothing like this flying-cage had ever before been seen in New York; thousands and thousands of men, women, and children thronged the lawn about the flying-cage all day long.

By night, also, the effect was wonderful; the electric lights among the foliage broke out; the great downy-winged moths, which had been asleep all day while the butterflies flitted through the sunshine, now came out to display their crimson or peacock-spotted wings, and the butterflies folded their wings and went to bed for the night.

The public was enchanted, the authorities of the Bronx proud and delighted; all apparently was happiness and harmony. Except that nobody offered me the Carnegie medal.

I was sitting one morning in my office, which, as I have said, separated the offices of Dr. Quint and Professor Boomly, when there came a loud rapping on my door, and, at my invitation, Dr. Quint bustled in—a little, meagre, excitable, near-sighted man with pointed mustaches and a fleck of an imperial smudging his lower lip.

"Last week," he began angrily, "young Jones arrived from Singapore bringing me the eggs of Erebia astarte, the great Silver Moon butterfly. Attempts to destroy them have been made. Last night I left them in a breeding-cage on my desk. Has anybody been in there?"

"I don't know," I said. "What has happened?"

"I found an ichneumon fly in the cage yesterday!" he shouted; "and this morning the eggs have either shrunk to half their size or else the eggs of another species have been secretly substituted for them and the Silver Moon eggs stolen! Has he been in there?"

"Who?" I asked, pretending to misunderstand.

"He!" demanded Quint fiercely. "If he has I'll kill him some day."

He meant his one-time friend, Dr. Boomly. Alas!

"For heaven's sake, why are you two perpetually squabbling?" I asked wearily. "You used to be inseparable friends. Why can't you make up?"

"Because I've come to know him. That's why! I have unmasked this—this Borgia—this Machiavelli—this monster of duplicity! Matters are approaching a point where something has got to be done short of murder. I've stood all his envy and jealousy and cheap imputations and hints and contemptible innuendoes that I'm going to—"

He stopped short, glaring at the doorway, which had suddenly been darkened by the vast bulk of Professor Boomly—a figure largely abdominal but majestic—like the massive butt end of an elephant. For the rest, he had a rather insignificant and peevish face and a melancholy mustache that usually looked damp.

"Mr. Smith," he said to me, in his thin, high, sarcastic voice—a voice incongruously at variance with his bulk—"has anybody had the infernal impudence to enter my room and nose about my desk?"

"Yes, I have!" replied Quint excitedly. "I've been in your room. What of it? What about it?"

Boomly permitted his heavy-lidded eyes to rest on Quint for a moment, then, turning to me:

"I want a patent lock put on my door. Will you speak to Professor Farrago?"

"I want one put on mine, too!" cried Quint. "I want a lock put on my door which will keep envious, dull-minded, mentally broken-down, impertinent, and fat people out of my office!"

Boomly flushed heavily:

"Fat?" he repeated, glaring at Quint. "Did you say 'fat?'"

"Yes, fat—intellectually and corporeally fat! I want that kind of individual kept out. I don't trust them. I'm afraid of them. Their minds are atrophied. They are unmoral, possibly even criminal! I don't want them in my room snooping about to see what I have and what I'm doing. I don't want them to sneak in, eaten up with jealousy and envy, and try to damage the eggs of the Silver Moon butterfly because the honour and glory of hatching them would probably procure for me the Carnegie Educational Medal—"

"Why, you little, dried-up, protoplasmic atom!" burst out Boomly, his face suffused with passion, "Are you insinuating that I have any designs on your batch of eggs?"

"It's my belief," shouted Quint, "that you want that medal yourself, and that you put an ichneumon fly in my breeding-cage in hopes it would sting the eggs of the Silver Moon."

"If you found an ichneumon fly there," retorted Boomly, "you probably hatched it in mistake for a butterfly!" And he burst into a peal of contemptuous laughter, but his little, pig-like eyes under the heavy lids were furious.

"I now believe," said Quint, trembling with rage, "that you have criminally substituted a batch of common Plexippus eggs for the Silver Moon eggs I had in my breeding-cage! I believe you are sufficiently abandoned to do it!"

"Ha! Ha!" retorted Boomly scornfully. "I don't believe you ever had anything in your breeding-cage except a few clothes moths and cockroaches!"

Quint began to dance:

"You did take them!" he yelled; "and you left me a bunch of milkweed butterflies' eggs! Give me my eggs or I shall violently assault you!"

"Assault your grandmother!" remarked Boomly, with unscientific brevity. "What do you suppose I want of your ridiculous eggs? Haven't I enough eggs of Heliconius salome hatching to give me the Carnegie medal if I want it?"

"The Silver Moon eggs are unique!" cried Quint. "You know it! You know that if they hatch, pupate, and become perfect insects that I shall certainly be awarded—"

"You'll be awarded the Matteawan medal," remarked Boomly with venom.

Quint ran at him with a half-suppressed howl, his momentum carrying him halfway up Professor Boomly's person. Then, losing foothold, he fell to the floor and began to kick in the general direction of Professor Boomly. It was a sorrowful sight to see these two celebrated scientists panting, mauling, scuffling and punching each other around the room, tables and chairs and scrapbaskets flying in every direction, and I mounted on the window-sill horrified, speechless, trying to keep clear of the revolving storm centre.

"Where are my Silver Moon eggs!" screamed Dr. Quint. "Where are my eggs that Jones brought me from Singapore—you entomological robber! You've got 'em somewhere! If you don't give 'em up I'll find means to destroy you!"

"You insignificant pair of maxillary palpi!" bellowed Professor Boomly, galloping after Dr. Quint as he dodged around my desk. "I'll pull off those antennæ you call whiskers if I can get hold of em-"

Dr. Quint's threatened mustaches bristled as he fled before the elephantine charge of Professor Boomly—once again around my desk, then out into the hall, where I heard the door of his office slam, and Boomly, gasping, panting, breathing vengeance outside, and vowing to leave Quint quite whiskerless when he caught him.

It was a painful scene for scientists to figure in or to gaze upon. Profoundly shocked and upset, I locked up the anthropological department offices and went out into the Park, where the sun was shining and a gentle June wind stirred the trees.

Too completely upset to do any more work that day, I wandered about amid the gaily dressed crowds at hazard; sometimes I contemplated the monkeys; sometimes gazed sadly upon the seals. They dashed and splashed and raced round and round their tank, or crawled up on the rocks, craned their wet, sleek necks, and barked— houp! houp! houp!

For luncheon I went over to the Rolling Stone Restaurant. There was a very pretty girl there—an unusually pretty girl—or perhaps it was one of those days on which every girl looked unusually pretty to me. There are such days.

Her voice was exquisite when she spoke. She said:

"We have, today, corned beef hash, fried ham and eggs, liver and bacon—" but let that pass, too.

I took my tea very weak; by that time I learned that her name was Mildred Case; that she had been a private detective employed in a department store, and that her duties had been to nab wealthy ladies who forgot to pay for objects usually discovered in their reticules, bosoms, and sometimes in their stockings.

But the confinement of indoor work had been too much for Mildred Case, and the only outdoor job she could find was the position of lady waitress in the rustic Rolling Stone Inn.

She was very, very beautiful, or perhaps it was one of those days—but let that pass, too.

"You are the great Mr. Percy Smith, Curator of the Anthropological Department, are you not?" she asked shyly.

"Yes," I said modestly; and, to slightly rebuke any superfluous pride in me, I paraphrased with becoming humility, pointing upward: "but remember, Mildred, there is One greater than I."

"Mr. Carnegie?" she nodded innocently. That was true, too. I let it go at that.

We chatted: she mentioned Professor Boomly and Dr. Quint, gently deploring the rupture of their friendship. Both gentlemen, in common with the majority of the administration personnel, were daily customers at the Rolling Stone Inn. I usually took my lunch from my boarding-house to my office, being too busy to go out for mere nourishment.

That is why I had hitherto missed Mildred Case.

"Mildred," I said, "I do not believe it can be wholesome for a man to eat sandwiches while taking minute measurements of defunct monkeys. Also, it is not a fragrant pastime. Hereafter I shall lunch here."

"It will be a pleasure to serve you," said that unusually—there I go again! It was an unusually beautiful day in June. Which careful, exact, and scientific statement, I think ought to cover the subject under consideration.

After luncheon I sadly selected a five-cent cigar; and, as I hesitated, lingering over the glass case, undecided still whether to give full rein to this contemplated extravagance, I looked up and found her beautiful grey eyes gazing into mine.

"What gentle thoughts are yours, Mildred?" I said softly.

"The cigar you have selected," she murmured, "is fly-specked."

Deeply touched that this young girl should have cared—that she should have expressed her solicitude so modestly, so sweetly, concerning the maculatory condition of my cigar, I thanked her and purchased, for the same sum, a packet of cigarettes.

That was going somewhat far for me. I had never in all my life even dreamed of smoking a cigarette. To a reserved, thoughtful, and scientific mind there is, about a packet of cigarettes, something undignified, something vaguely frolicsome.

When I paid her for them I felt as though, for the first time in my life, I had let myself go.

Oddly enough, in this uneasy feeling of gaiety and abandon, a curious sensation of exhilaration persisted.

We had quite a merry little contretemps when I tried to light my cigarette and the match went out, and then she struck another match, and we both laughed, and that match was extinguished by her breath.

Instantly I quoted: "'Her breath was like the new-mown hay—'"

"Mr. Smith!" she said, flushing slightly.

"'Her eyes,' I quoted, 'were like the stars at even!'"

"You don't mean my eyes, do you?"

I took a puff at my unlighted cigarette. It also smelled like recently mown hay. I felt that I was slipping my cables and heading toward an unknown and tempestuous sea.

"What time are you free, Mildred?" I asked, scarcely recognising my own voice in such reckless apropos.

She shyly informed me.

I struck a match, relighted my cigarette, and took one puff. That was sufficient: I was adrift. I realised it, trembled internally, took another puff.

"If," said I carelessly, "on your way home you should chance to stroll along the path beyond the path that leads to the path which—"

I paused, checked by her bewildered eyes. We both blushed.

"Which way do you usually go home?" I asked, my ears afire.

She told me. It was a suitably unfrequented path.

So presently I strolled thither; and seated myself under the trees in a bosky dell.

Now, there is a quality in boskiness not inappropriate to romantic thoughts. Boskiness, cigarettes, a soft afternoon in June, the hum of bees, and the distant barking of the seals, all these were delicately blending to inspire in me a bashful sentiment.

A specimen of Papilio turnus, di-morphic form, Glaucus, alighted near me; I marked its flight with scientific indifference. Yet it is a rare species in Bronx Park.

A mock-orange bush was in snowy bloom behind me; great bunches of wistaria hung over the rock beside me.

The combination of these two exquisite perfumes seemed to make the boskiness more bosky.

There was an unaccustomed and sportive lightness to my step when I rose to meet Mildred, where she came loitering along the shadow-dappled path.

She seemed surprised to see me.

She thought it rather late to sit down, but she seated herself. I talked to her enthusiastically about anthropology. She was so interested that after a while she could scarcely keep still, moving her slim little feet restlessly, biting her pretty lower lip, shifting her position—all certain symptoms of an interest in science which even approached excitement.

Warmed to the heart by her eager and sympathetic interest in the noble science so precious, so dear to me, I took her little hand to soothe and quiet her, realizing that she might become overexcited as

I described the pituitary body and why its former functions had become atrophied until the gland itself was nearly obsolete.

So intense her interest had been that she seemed a little tired. I decided to give adequate material support to her spinal process. It seemed to rest and soothe her. I don't remember that she said anything except: "Mr. Smith!" I don't recollect what we were saying when she mentioned me by name rather abruptly.

The afternoon was wonderfully still and calm. The month was June.

After a while—quite a while—some little time in point of accurate fact—she detected the sound of approaching footsteps.

I remember that she was seated at the opposite end of the bench, rather feverishly occupied with her hat and her hair, when young Jones came hastily along the path, caught sight of us, halted, turned violently red—being a shy young man—but instead of taking himself off, he seemed to recover from a momentary paralysis.

"Mr. Smith!" he said sharply. "Professor Boomly has disappeared; there's a pool of blood on his desk; his coat, hat, and waistcoat are lying on the floor, the room is a wreck, and Dr. Quint is in there tearing up the carpet and behaving like a madman. We think he suddenly went insane and murdered Professor Boomly. What is to be done?"

Horrified, I had risen at his first word. And now, as I understood the full purport of his dreadful message, my hair stirred under my hat and I gazed at him, appalled.

"What is to be done?" he demanded. "Shall I telephone for the police?"

"Do you actually believe," I faltered, "that this unfortunate man has murdered Boomly?"

"I don't know. I looked over the transom, but I couldn't see Professor Boomly. Dr. Quint has locked the door."

"And he's tearing up the carpet?"

"Like a lunatic. I didn't want to call in the police until I'd asked you. Such a scandal in Bronx Park would be a frightful thing for us all—" He hesitated, looked around, coldly, it seemed to me, at Mildred Case. "A scandal," he repeated, "is scarcely what might be expected among a harmonious and earnest band of seekers after scientific knowledge. Is it, Mil—Miss Case?"

Now, I don't know why Mildred should have blushed. There was nothing that I could see in this young man's question to embarrass her.

Preoccupied, still confused by the shock of this terrible news, I looked at Jones and at Mildred; and they were staring rather oddly at each other.

I said: "If this affair turns out to be as ghastly as it seems to promise, we'll have to call in a detective. I'll go back immediately—"

"Why not take me, also?" asked Mildred Case, quietly.

"What?" I asked, looking at her.

"Why not, Mr. Smith? I was once a private detective."

Surprised at the suggestion, I hesitated.

"If you desire to keep this matter secret—if you wish to have it first investigated privately and quietly—would it not be a good idea to let me use my professional knowledge before you call in the police? Because as soon as the police are summoned all hope of avoiding publicity is at an end."

She spoke so sensibly, so quietly, so modestly, that her offer of assistance deeply impressed me.

As for young Jones, he looked at her steadily in that odd, chilling manner, which finally annoyed me. There was no need of his being snobbish because this very lovely and intelligent young girl happened to be a waitress at the Rolling Stone Inn.

"Come," I said unsteadily, again a prey to terrifying emotions; "let us go to the Administration Building and learn how matters stand. If this affair is as terrible as I fear it to be, science has received the deadliest blow ever dealt it since Cagliostro perished."

As we three strode hastily along the path in the direction of the Administration Building, I took that opportunity to read these two youthful fellow beings a sermon on envy, jealousy, and coveteousness.

"See," said I, "to what a miserable condition the desire for notoriety and fame has brought two learned and enthusiastic delvers in the vineyard of endeavor! The mad desire for the Carnegie medal completely turned the hitherto perfectly balanced brains of these devoted disciples of Science. Envy begat envy, jealousy begat jealousy, pride begat pride, hatred begat hatred—"

"It's like that book in the Bible where everybody begat everybody else," said Mildred seriously.

At first I thought she had made an apt and clever remark; but on thinking it over I couldn't quite see its relevancy. I turned and looked into her sweet face. Her eyes were dancing with brilliancy and her sensitive lips quivered. I feared, she was near to tears from the reaction of the shock. Had Jones not been walking with us—but let that go, too.

We were now entering the Administration Building, almost running; and as soon as we came to the closed door of Dr. Quint's room, I could hear a commotion inside—desk drawers being pulled out and their contents dumped, curtains being jerked from their rings, an unmistakable sound indicating the ripping up of a carpet—and through all this din the agitated scuffle of footsteps.

I rapped on the door. No notice taken. I rapped and knocked and called in a low, distinct voice.

Suddenly I recollected I had a general pass-key on my ring which unlocked any door in the building. I nodded to Jones and to Mildred to stand aside, then, gently fitting the key, I suddenly pushed out the key which remained on the inside, turned the lock, and flung open the door.

A terrible sight presented itself: Dr. Quint, hair on end, both mustaches pulled out, shirt, cuffs, and white waistcoat smeared with blood, knelt amid the general wreckage on the floor, in the act of ripping up the carpet.

"Doctor!" I cried in a trembling voice. "What have you done to Professor Boomly?"

He paused in his carpet ripping and looked around at us with a terrifying laugh.

"I've settled him!" he said. "If you don't want to get all over dust you'd better keep out—"

"Quint!" I cried. "Are you crazy?"

"Pretty nearly. Let me alone—"

"Where is Boomly!" I demanded in a tragic voice. "Where is your old friend, Billy Boomly? Where is he, Quint? And what does that mean—that pool of blood on the floor? Whose is it?"

"It's Bill's," said Quint, coolly ripping up another breadth of carpet and peering under it.

"What!" I exclaimed. "Do you admit that?"

"Certainly I admit it. I told him I'd terminate him if he meddled with my Silver Moon eggs."

"You mean to say that you shed blood—the blood of your old friend—merely because he meddled with a miserable batch of butterfly's eggs?" I asked, astounded.

"I certainly did shed his blood for just that particular thing! And listen; you're in my way—you're standing on a part of the carpet which I want to tear up. Do you mind moving?"

Such cold-blooded calmness infuriated me. I sprang at Quint, seized him, and shouted to Jones to tie his hands behind him with the blood-soaked handkerchief which lay on the floor.

At first, while Jones and I were engaged in the operation of securing the wretched man, Quint looked at us both as though surprised; then he grew angry and asked us what the devil we were about.

"Those who shed blood must answer for it!" I said solemnly.

"What? What's the matter with you?" he demanded in a rage.

"Shed blood? What if I did? What's that to you? Untie this handkerchief, you unmentionable idiot!"

I looked at Jones:

"His mind totters," I said hoarsely.

"What's that!" cried Quint, struggling to get off the chair whither I had pushed him: but with my handkerchief we tied his ankles to the rung of the chair, heedless of his attempts to kick us, and sprang back out of range.

"Now," I said, "what have you done with the poor victim of your fury? Where is he? Where is all that remains of Professor Boomly?"

"Boomly? I don't know where he is. How the devil should I know?"

"Don't lie," I said solemnly.

"Lie! See here, Smith, when I get out of this chair I'll settle you, too—"

"Quint! There is another and more terrible chair which awaits such criminals as you!"

"You old fluff!" he shouted. "I'll knock your head off, too. Do you understand? I'll attend to you as I attended to Boomly—"

"Assassin!" I retorted calmly. "Only an alienist can save you now. In this awful moment—"

A light touch on my arm interrupted me, and, a trifle irritated, as any man might be when checked in the full flow of eloquence, I turned to find Mildred at my elbow.

"Let me talk to him," she said in a quiet voice. "Perhaps I may not irritate him as you seem to."

"Very well," I said. "Jones and I are here as witnesses." And I folded my arms in an attitude not, perhaps, unpicturesque.

"Dr. Quint," said Mildred in her soft, agreeable voice, and actually smiling slightly at the self-confessed murderer, "is it really true that you are guilty of shedding the blood of Professor Boomly?"

"It is," said Quint, coolly.

She seemed rather taken aback at that, but presently recovered her equanimity.

"Why?" she asked gently.

"Because he attempted a most hellish crime!" yelled Quint.

"W-what crime?" she asked faintly.

"I'll tell you. He wanted the Carnegie medal, and he knew it would be given to me if I could incubate and hatch my batch of Silver Moon butterfly eggs. He realised well enough that his Heliconian eggs were not as valuable as my Silver Moon eggs. So first he sneaked in here and put an ichneumon fly in my breeding-cage. And next he stole the Silver Moon eggs and left in their place some common Plexippus eggs, thinking that because they were very similar I would not notice the substitution.

"I did notice it! I charged him with that cataclysmic outrage. He laughed. We came into personal collision. He chased me into my room."

Panting, breathless with rage at the memory of the morning's defeat which I had witnessed, Quint glared at me for a moment. Then he jerked his head toward Mildred:

"As soon as he went to luncheon—Boomly, I mean—I climbed over that transom and dropped into this room. I had been hunting for ten minutes before I found my Silver Moon eggs hidden under the carpet. So I pocketed them, climbed back over the transom, and went to my room."

He paused dramatically, staring from one to another of us:

"Boomly was there!" he said slowly.

"Where?" asked Mildred with a shudder.

"In my room. He had picked the lock. I told him to get out! He went. I shouted after him that I had recovered the Silver Moon eggs and that I should certainly be awarded the Carnegie medal.

"Then that monster in human form laughed a horrible laugh, avowing himself guilty of a crime still more hideous than the theft of the Silver Moon eggs! Do you know what he had done?"

"W-what?" faltered Mildred.

"He had stolen from cold storage and had concealed the leaves of the Bimba bush, brought from Singapore to feed the Silver Moon caterpillars! That's what Boomly had done!

"And my Silver Moon eggs had already begun to hatch!!! And my caterpillars would starve!!!!"

His voice ended in a yell; he struggled on his chair until it nearly upset.

"You lunatic!" I shouted. "Was that a reason for spilling the blood of a human being!"

"It was reason enough for me!"

"Madman!"

"Let me loose! He's hidden those leaves somewhere or other! I've torn this place to pieces looking for them. I've got to find them, I tell you—"

Mildred went to the infuriated entomologist and laid a firm hand on his shoulder:

"Listen," she said: "how do you know that Professor Boomly has not concealed these Bimba leaves on his own person?"

Quint ceased his contortions and gaped at her.

"I never thought of that," he said.

"What have you done with him?" she asked, very pale.

"I tell you, I don't know."

"You must know what you did with him," she insisted.

Quint shook his head impatiently, apparently preoccupied with other thoughts. We stood watching him in silence until he looked up and became conscious of our concentrated gaze.

"My caterpillars are starving," he began violently. "I haven't anything else they'll eat. They feed only on the Bimba leaf. They won't eat anything else. It's a well-known fact that they won't. Why, in Johore, where they came from, they'll travel miles over the ground to find a Bimba bush—"

"What!" exclaimed Mildred.

"Certainly—miles! They'd starve sooner than eat anything except Bimba leaves. If there's a bush within twenty miles they'll find it—"

"Wait," said Mildred quietly. "Where are these starving caterpillars?"

"In a glass jar in my pocket—here! What the devil are you doing!" For the girl had dexterously slipped the glass jar from his coat pocket and was holding it up to the light.

Inside it were several dozen tiny, dark caterpillars, some resting disconsolately on the sides of the glass, some hungrily travelling over the bottom in pitiful and hopeless quest of nourishment.

Heedless of the shouts and threats of Dr. Quint, the girl calmly uncorked the jar, took on her slender forefinger a single little caterpillar, replaced the cork, and, kneeling down, gently disengaged the caterpillar. It dropped upon the floor, remained motionless for a moment, then, turning, began to travel rapidly toward the doorway behind us.

"Now," she said, "if poor Professor Boomly really has concealed these Bimba leaves upon his own person, this little caterpillar, according to Dr. Quint, is certain to find those leaves."

Overcome with excitement and admiration for this intelligent and unusually beautiful girl, I seized her hands and congratulated her.

"Murder," said I to the miserable Quint, "will out! This infant caterpillar shall lead us to that dark and secret spot where you had hoped to conceal the horrid evidence of your guilt. Three things have undone you—a caterpillar replete with mysterious instinct, a humble bunch of Bimba leaves, and the marvellous intelligence of this young and lovely girl. Madman, your hour has struck!"

He looked at me in a dazed sort of way, as though astonishment had left him unable to articulate. But I had become tired of his violence and his shouts and yells; so I asked Jones for his handkerchief, and, before Quint knew what I was up to I had tied it over his mouth.

He became a brilliant purple, but all he could utter was a furious humming, buzzing noise.

Meanwhile, Jones had opened the door; the little caterpillar, followed by Mildred and myself, continued to hustle along as though he knew quite well where he was going.

Down the hallway he went in undulating haste, past my door, we all following in silent excitement as we discovered that, parallel to the caterpillar's course, ran a gruesome trail of blood drops.

And when the little creature turned and made straight for the door of Professor Farrago, our revered chief, the excitement among us was terrific.

The caterpillar halted; I gently tried the door; it was open.

Instantly the caterpillar crossed the threshold, wriggling forward at top speed. We followed, peering fearfully around us. Nobody was visible.

Could Quint have dragged his victim here? By Heaven, he had! For the caterpillar was travelling straight under the lounge upon which Professor Farrago was accustomed to repose after luncheon, and, dropping on one knee, I saw a fat foot partly protruding from under the shirred edges of the fringed drapery.

"He's there!" I whispered, in an awed voice to the others.

"Courage, Miss Case! Try not to faint."

Jones turned and looked at her with that same odd expression; then he went over to where she stood and coolly passed one arm around her waist.

"Try not to faint, Mildred," he said. "It might muss your hair."

It was a strange thing to say, but I had no time then to analyze it, for I had seized the fat foot which partly protruded from under the sofa, clad in a low-cut congress gaiter and a white sock.

And then I nearly fainted, for instead of the dreadful, inert resistance of lifeless clay, the foot wriggled and tried to kick at me.

"Help!" came a thin but muffled voice. "Help! Help, in the name of Heaven!"

"Boomly!" I cried, scarcely believing my ears.

"Take that man away, Smith!" whimpered Boomly. "He's a devil! He'll murder me! He made my nose bleed all over everything!"

"Boomly! You're not dead!"

"Yes, I am!" he whined. "I'm dead enough to suit me. Keep that little lunatic off—that's all I ask. He can have his Carnegie medal for all I care, only tie him up somewhere—"

"Professor Boomly!" cried Mildred excitedly. "Have you any Bimba leaves concealed about your person?"

"Yes, I have," he said sulkily. There came a hitch of the fat foot, a heavy scuffling sound, heavy panting, and then, skittering out across the floor came a flat, sealed parcel.

"There you are," he said; "now, let me alone until that fiend has gone home."

"He won't attack you again," I said. "Come out."

But Professor Boomly flatly declined to stir.

I looked at the parcel: it was marked: "Bimba leaves; Johore."

With a sigh of unutterable relief, I picked up the ravenous little caterpillar, placed him on the packet, and turned to go. And didn't.

It is a very sickening fact I have now to record. But to a scientist all facts are sacred, sickening or otherwise.

For what I caught a glimpse of, just outside the door in the hallway, was Jones kissing Mildred Case. And being shyly indemnified for his trouble with a gentle return in kind. Both his arms were around her waist; both her hands rested upon his shoulders; and, as I looked—but let it pass!—let it pass.

Deliberately I fished in my pocket, found my packet of cigarettes, lighted one.

Tobacco diffugiunt mordaces curae et laetificat cor hominis!

THE END